Break Away 2

POWER FORWARD

OTHER BOOKS BY SYLVAIN HOTTE

Break Away 1, Jessie on my mind (Baraka Books)
The Darhan Series (2006-2008)
Darhan, La fée du lac Baïkal
Darhan, Les chemins de la guerre
Darhan, La jeune fille sans visage
Darhan, La malédiction
Darhan, Les métamorphoses
Darhan, L'esprit de Kökötchü
Darhan, L'empereur Océan
Darhan, Le Voyageur

Miguel Torres (1998)

Le chagrin des étoiles (2008)

Les fistons (2008)

The *Break Away* series are the first books by Sylvain Hotte to
appear in English.

Sylvain Hotte

Break Away 2
POWER FORWARD

Translated by Casey Roberts

Baraka
Books
Montreal

Originally published as *Aréna 2. Attaquant de puissance*
© 2009 by Les Éditions des Intouchables

Publié avec l'autorisation des Éditions des Intouchables, Montréal, Québec, Canada

Translation Copyright © Baraka Books 2012

Cover by Folio Infographie
Book design by Folio Infographie
Translated by Casey Roberts

Legal Deposit, 2nd quarter, 2012
Bibliothèque et Archives nationales du Québec
Library and Archives Canada

Published by Baraka Books

6977, rue Lacroix
Montréal, Québec H4E 2V4
Telephone: 514 808-8504
info@barakabooks.com
www.barakabooks.com
Printed and bound in Quebec

Trade Distribution & Returns
Canada
LitDistCo
1-800-591-6250; ordering@litdistco.ca

United States
Independent Publishers Group
1-800-888-4741 (IPG1);
orders@ipgbook.com

Baraka Books acknowledges the generous support of its publishing program from the Société de développement des entreprises culturelles du Québec (SODEC) and the Canada Council for the Arts.

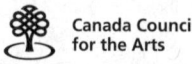

We acknowledge the financial support of the Government of Canada, through the National Translation Program for Book Publishing for our translation activities.

Chapter 1

I can't remember ever being so tired in all my life. My legs, dead. My thighs, on fire. My feet were so swollen that they popped right out of my running shoes. The July sun pounded down, relentless. Dust and sand whipped my face, driven in gusts by the east wind that swept clouds of spray across the choppy water. And behind me, going on and on forever, Larry's voice pushing me on, telling me never give up.

Come St. Jean Baptiste Day, in late June, my training routine looked like this: up at 5 a.m. then run five kilometres along Highway 138. Next, lift weights out in the garage, then a huge breakfast. That's how my workday started. Then I would head up to Lake Matamek. The government had given my father money to plant 120,000 trees. Between the two of us, we could handle it, he figured. The only thing is, 120,000 trees is a lot of trees. The days were long and hard. I'd meet up with him on the other side of the lake, on his hunting territory, the *natau-assi,* around 9:30 a.m. Then I'd work like a madman, planting trees like there was no tomorrow, hoping to transplant at least a thousand before three o'clock in the afternoon. More than a few times I'd be eating lunch, sandwich in one hand and shovel in the other, digging a hole for the next seedling. I ate more than my share of mud and dried leaves!

Along about three in the afternoon, Larry would show up on his quad. You could hear the big Grizzly roaring like an American bomber at 20,000 feet. Larry was on the small side; he eked out a living doing summer jobs. The previous summer, he lost his job at the tourism office when he called a couple from Ottawa "morons" because they were looking for the Percé Rock on the North Shore of the St. Lawrence. But this year, he didn't have to go looking for another lousy job like he usually pulled down between hockey seasons. My father took part of the transplanting money and put him on salary as my personal trainer. As soon as he laid hands on what for him was a substantial amount of money, Larry, who wasn't accustomed to cash on hand and couldn't even remember the last time he'd had four digits in his bank account, went out and bought himself a big and nasty ATV, a monster machine with a heated seat and handlebars, a winch in the front and a hitch in the rear, and support struts all the way around. Larry lived in a semi-basement apartment at Mrs. Fontaine's, next door to the church. He was a poor man, he had nothing, but now he could pull a 45-footer out of the woods with that all-terrain of his. And that had to count for something.

"What is that thing, Larry?" asked my father, the first time he showed up with his flashy machine.

"It's my Grizzly," he said proudly, his eyes squinting behind his blue-tinted lenses.

"So I see. You can pay an arm and a leg for one of those babies."

"Don't you worry about me. I'll work things out."

And he kept on smiling, one hand on his thigh, the other on the handlebars, proud as a bush pilot flying a supersonic jet.

He would always "work things out," like he said. You could bet on it. Larry always managed to work things out. Maybe not always in the best way, though. I thought I heard he was going through his second bankruptcy. Nothing to be sneezed at. Truth is, that thick-headed attitude of his just showed he didn't really give a damn. Because even more than shelling out big bucks on fifty-three inch plasma TVs, trips down South, or a crazy huge quad that he absolutely didn't need, there was really only one thing that truly mattered to him: hockey. And he wouldn't let me forget it every time we met for my end-of-the-day work-out: I was going to be the best player at the Quebec City junior team camp. Except I wasn't a quad. I had my limits.

Every day, rain or shine, we rode out past Pointe-Noire to a huge beach more than five kilometres long and dotted with dunes. I'd run out and back barefoot, and anybody that's ever run on sand knows it takes twice the effort. And if I ever, even for one moment, swerved down to where the sand was wet, tamped down by the high tide, Larry would lean on the Grizzly's horn to drive me back on the soft stuff.

Usually I could handle this awful end-of-the-day jog, even if it made me want to puke and it didn't seem to make any sense. Not this time; I was wasted. One more sprint under these conditions and my heart would explode. My lungs were killing me. I stopped to catch my breath, bent over, hands on my knees.

"Don't give up, McKenzie. You're not done."

"Sorry, man. I can't cut it."

"Man? What do you mean you can't cut it? When some 19 or 20-year-old smacks you around in training camp, you're going to go see the coach and tell him, 'I can't cut it'? That'll be just great."

"Give me a break, Larry. It's hot as hell. I planted 15,000 trees today."

"In the NHL ..."

"There won't be any NHL if I have a heart attack at sixteen."

Perched on the seat of his quad, he ran his hand through his long red hair and then took off his glasses, blowing the sand off his lenses.

"Hmm. Okay. Take five."

My legs were so shaky I couldn't bend them to sit. I let myself fall on my butt and sank into the sand. The weather was spoiling. The sun disappeared behind a bank of dark grey clouds; the wind turned chilly. Shivers ran up and down my sweat-drenched body.

I took a few sips of water; gradually my gasping breath and racing heart returned to normal. But no sooner had I begun to relax when I heard Larry telling me not to take too long a break. The more I waited the harder it would be to finish my run. I knew he was right. If I sat there one minute longer I'd stiffen up so much I couldn't take another step. I gritted my teeth and took off at a trot, like a horse on his last legs.

Using my hands, I scrambled up a huge sand dune, while Larry drove around it on his quad. At that moment I heard what sounded like firecrackers popping. What it was, was an engine humming at a high pitch and backfiring like crazy. There was only one halfwit I knew who could be making sounds like that. Off in the distance, beyond the tall dune from which I could see the whole expanse of the Pointe-Noire beach, I saw a cloud of dust moving with the wind. Then, a purple vehicle would briefly appear and disappear as it zigzagged its way between the dunes. I recognized it: Mike and his dune buggy. And he was heading my way.

I rolled all the way down to the bottom of the big dune. Like a frightened animal, I ran like I was being pursued by a terrible predator from another planet. It was no use. I was no match for the monster. Like out of some safari, Mike caught up with me and began riding circles around me, throwing up a thick cloud of blinding sand. I pulled my shirt up over my face and ran down to the water where the sand was wet. Mike was cracking up at the terrified look on my face. Grinning from ear to ear, he switched off the purple monster with its red and orange vinyl flames. He was high on the speed and the salt air, but also because it was pay-back time for last winter's humiliation at Lake Matamek.

"Hey champ!" he said.

"Hi Mike. How's it going?"

"Not bad, as you can see," he said, patting his buggy. "Stéphane's going out fishing tomorrow. He wants to know if you're on."

I would have liked to have gone out on Stéphane Leblanc's fishing boat. Most likely he'd be after mackerel. As you reel them in with the roller, you can see the open mouths of the fish through the steel scupper rails before they tumble into the plastic tubs. We bring 'em in with spinners: impressive and kind of yucky. We'd probably have dragged a few lines for halibut too. They can be huge and they're delicious. Unfortunately, I only had Sunday off. And behind me, even if I couldn't see him, I could feel Larry shaking his head from right to left telling me "no."

"No can do, Mike. Gotta work out."

"Sure," he goes, putting his hat back on. "Don't over-train, or you'll end up like friggin' Courchesne. I saw him just this morning comin' out of the Baie-Comeau gym. His arms were as big as my head. Unreal!"

"Courchesne" is my friend Tommy. Last spring, at the end of the season, Larry put him on the first line with me. That worked out great. And the team won the championship.

The armchair coaches claim that playing on the top line with Félix and me was the reason for Tommy's success in the finals; otherwise, Shawinigan would never have drafted him. Félix has a lot more talent but he's still too small and not ready for the major juniors. Tommy's beefier, which is what made the difference.

Like me, he trains hard. But he spends almost all his time in the Baie-Comeau gym. And he's bulked up big. Real big. Larry doesn't go for that. Tommy does too much weightlifting and not enough cardio. By the time he gets to camp he'll be too heavy, he won't be able to keep up.

Mike waved goodbye and gunned the dune buggy. What a getaway! The purple monster dug two deep furrows in the wet sand, which quickly flooded with sea-water. I watched him head off into the distance, big Mike on his machine, skipping over the dunes like a jackrabbit. I felt crappy. It wasn't just missing the fishing trip with Leblanc; it wasn't even the sand that Mike's buggy had just shockingly thrown into my face. Neither was it hearing that Tommy was puffing up, lifting more and more weight every day. What it was, was that Mike had just shown up wearing a Boston Bruins hat, which meant I was going to have to teach him another lesson. How? I didn't know. But I was definitely going to think of something.

The rain began to fall on Pointe-Noire. So hard that it dashed even Larry's determination. He motioned me to climb onto his big Grizzly and we drove around the point, beneath the tall black spruces that give the place its name. The sea was swelling and the waves were breaking on the reef three kilometres offshore. The deluge didn't last long, but a minute was enough to soak us to the bone. Then, turning his back on the trail that would have brought us directly into town, Larry veered onto the 138 and we drove at full speed back to my place. I thought I was a crazy driver. But my coach was even crazier. I wouldn't go so far as to say I was scared, but I wasn't very comfortable either. Especially when I felt the rear-end of the four-wheeler lifting off the road surface every time we went around a turn, giving us the impression that we were destined for the ditch. I imagined myself sliding fifty feet on the asphalt feeling all my skin scraping off on the gravel, and then getting squashed by an eighteen wheeler. Not a pretty thought. But nothing happened. I got home alive. I said goodbye to Larry who, true to form, told me to get to bed early and not hang out with any girls. Don't worry, I told him, and watched as he steered the Grizzly back onto the road, this time rolling slowly along the shoulder.

I realized that Larry had really wanted to give me a scare. Like maybe I could jump up on his machine under exceptional circumstances such as the storm. But next time, I'd be back to running, same as always. No rest for soldiers. The warrior keeps himself in a state of constant readiness, so that in battle he's ready to fight to his full potential, thereby increasing his chances of victory. It was the kind of crap he probably read in his military strategy or coaching books, ideas that got all mixed up somewhere behind those thick smoky blue lenses of his.

I took a shower, massaging my aching thighs. Then I sat on my bed. My fingernails, even after I scrubbed them with a brush, were still dirty, encrusted with soil from tree planting. My father could have waited a year before starting planting. He had even mulled over the possibility. But Larry, who was never short of ways to make his charges suffer, had encouraged him to start right away. It was just what an athlete needed, he argued: rigorous, hard work to toughen the body. And the mind. Because the mind was what counted most, even more than talent or physical condition. And, for sure, my "mind" wasn't what you would call my biggest strength. Larry had made exactly that point, weighing his words to convince Louis, my father, to start me on the program during my first year in the juniors. But his sales pitch didn't really fool me. Most of all I'm thinking Larry already had a big Yamaha poster hanging on his wall with a close-up of the Grizzly 700 and he'd already figured it into his bear-hunting plans. Because, bear hunting—I don't know if you've ever known a bear hunter—let's just say those guys are "something else."

I thought it'd be a good idea if I said hello to Sylvie who had come home from work while I was in the shower. She was in the kitchen chopping carrots or celery. I thought maybe I'd ride up to Chez Lisette and see if some of my friends were hanging out there, maybe missing me. It was like I never saw anyone anymore. My Spartan training had pretty much wiped out my social life. But I was so tired, my body so heavy with fatigue, that it just seemed like my bed was the most perfect place to be in all the world. I stretched out on my back and jammed a pillow under my feet, as I sometimes like to do. I slept deeply, to the sound of rain hammering against the window.

When I awoke it was past 7:30. Sylvie came into my room like a blast of cold air. She yanked open the drapes and the orange light of the setting sun flooded in. Little specks of dust danced in the sunlight while I tried to rub the sleep out of my eyes. I groaned.

"It's too nice outside to be sleeping, champ."

"It was just raining."

"But now it's nice. I made some soup. Did your father tell you if he'd be home tonight?"

"I don't know."

"When you see him tomorrow, tell him he has to pay the electricity and phone bills."

All Louis really wanted was to get those 120,000 trees planted. He worked from sunrise to sunset and slept in his prospector tent most of the time, at least while he was at camp. I could already hear him growling like a bear when I told him he had to come on home to write some cheques for Hydro-Québec and Bell.

After downing a big bowl of soup and two sandwiches, I headed for the garage, munching a banana. The Skiroule was fast asleep under its dusty blanket. This time last summer, I'd have jumped on my Suzuki and gone up to the lake or down to the beach. But I was out of luck since my father had taken the quad to go work in the bush and I was on foot. I looked at the brand new dumbbells and the weight-lifting bench. My heart really wasn't in it, but I set up to do some 250-pound bench presses. After three repetitions I quit. I just couldn't get into it. Besides, I was burping up banana and it was grossing me out. I was reaching the end of my rope, what with running, weightlifting and tree planting. I wanted to get back on the ice. I wanted to skate. That's what I was made for. But Larry had turned a deaf ear and decided there wouldn't be any power skating before the end of July. He was making me wait, so that when I finally got the green light, I'd hit the ice in a frenzy, just a couple of weeks before training camp got underway. Another theory that he'd invented in that militarized world of his, where abstinence and desire make the warrior, the athlete, etc.

Feeling a bit blasé, I left the garage and I walked for a while down the 138. The sun hadn't quite set. The stars were out, but a long trail of pink and orange clouds still hung in the sky. Looking from one side of the road to the other, my hands in my pockets, kicking gravel onto the potholed asphalt, I wondered if I should head east and take the Mill Road up to the woods. Or follow the setting sun to the west, towards the village, and maybe grab some fries at Chez Lisette. But I didn't have a chance to tackle these highly existential questions. A rusty old black Comanche pickup was coming down the road. As soon as the driver recognized me, he swung off onto the shoulder. He braked on the gravel, coming to a stop one foot in front of me. It was Tommy.

"Hey, boss!" he said, opening the door for me.

I climbed in and sat down on the ripped imitation leather. It smelled like transmission oil and maple leaf cookies.

"How's it going, boss?"

Boss, what a joke. He had started calling me boss during the finals. Every time I said something on the ice before a faceoff, he snapped off his answer as if he was in the army with his signature "yes, boss." But he gave it everything he had. And we managed to net one to escape with the win. He'd scored 19 points in the finals; he was proud of himself and with good reason, finishing fourth among all scorers, behind Félix and a guy named Marcoux from Sept-Îles who skated faster than his own shadow and who had been drafted by Bathurst in New Brunswick.

With his disciplined approach, he would have benefitted from working with coaching-sergeant Larry, who had offered to design him a training program. Tommy had agreed, but only for on-ice workouts. His personal trainer, who was also his advisor and nutritionist, would be his cousin, the owner of the Baie-Comeau gym. The program seemed to have gotten results, at least as far as appearance was concerned. Because in less than three months, Tommy had become a different person. He wore blue jeans that were tight on his bulked-up thighs and a white shirt cut to show off his huge shoulders and muscular arms. Even his face had changed, becoming wider, his chin jutting and more angular. Whenever you looked at him, he was clenching his teeth and the muscles of his jaw were rippling. His neck was bigger too, with large veins that protruded when he clenched his teeth. For a while now, he had seemed overly nervous or even aggressive. And always in a sweat.

"Where're you off to?"

"I'm going to meet Karine," he said, clenching the biceps of his right arm.

"I thought you weren't seeing each other anymore."

"Nah. We're still cool. She's waiting for me with some friends at the restaurant. We're going to make a bonfire out at the point. Want to come?"

A bonfire at the point… That means a ton of people, music cranked up loud (which I hate right down on the water) and plenty of booze. Everybody would be offering me some. I'd be turning down beers just until I'd have had it with hearing people insist; finally I'd take one but only drink half of it. I had to work out tomorrow. I had trees to plant.

"I don't think so." "Come on. Let's go have some fun!"

"I've got to get up early tomorrow."

"Look, I train hard too. But that doesn't stop me from having a little fun. You've got to relax. What do you think the Habs do when they're not playing hockey? Do you think they go to bed early after eating their cookies and drinking their milk? Come on! What time do you get up?"

"I'm not sure exactly."

"What time do you get up at?" he insisted.

"Six o'clock."

"So, I get up at five," he told me. "I run 15 kilometres every morning. Then I lift weights at the gym. Run some more, lift some more weights. Does that stop me from having fun? No!"

And then Tommy began to growl. And he shook his fist at the highway. I said nothing, refusing to get sucked into his macho game. Good for him if he had an iron constitution. As for me, everything tired me out and all I could think of was sleeping. I had no desire to go to the point. But there was no point in arguing with him, or even in getting out of the truck, since the rusty old Comanche was already rolling down the road. Five minutes later, we turned into the parking lot at Chez Lisette.

Not many people had gathered at Pointe-Noire. True enough, a stiff cold wind was blowing down from the mountains, enough to discourage the faint hearted. There were only three cars, and now, Tommy's pickup hitting the beach with a bang, scattering people every which way. Real funny, he must have thought and guffawed, smacking the dash several times with his open hand. Karine, who was sitting up front with him, didn't say a word. But she was watching him out of the corner of her eye, as if she was afraid.

We joined the group around the driftwood fire. The wind that fanned the fast-burning fire swept fat sparks into the sky. The low flames licked the sea-sculpted driftwood, which looked like an animal roasting on a spit. Tommy, who had put in a new speaker system in his pickup, cranked up the music to the max. Too bad for anybody who'd been thinking about a relaxing evening. In fact, everyone was laid back except Tommy, who was getting more and more ridiculous with every beer he downed.

At Chez Lisette we had picked up Karine, Anna-Maria Escobar—a girl from South America who'd been living in our town for a number of years now—and Chloé, who laughed at everything. I let Tommy's girl-friend sit in the front seat with him, and jumped into the back with the other two girls. After which I didn't say much. Chloé and Anna-Maria were goofing around nonstop. They would say stupid things in a loud voice and laugh like nut cases. Me, I couldn't understand a word. It was like they spoke a language from another planet, from another universe even, no way for a guy like me to understand. It was girl talk.

When they noticed I wasn't paying them any attention, and avoiding them by trying to spot something interesting through the window of the fibreglass cab, they began asking me questions. Questions about anything and everything, which I answered like a goof, mumbling incoherent strings of words with a shrug, like it didn't matter anyway.

"Do you get off on planting trees?" asked Anna-Maria.

"Umm," I said.

"My father can't handle it anymore. Too much back pain."

When Anna-Maria's father began to work in our area I wasn't even born yet. He'd come every summer to plant trees for the Company. Back then, only foreigners and students would take those back-breaking, low-paying jobs.

Today, things are different.

It didn't look quite that way to Anna-Maria's father. He saved every penny, and ended up buying an old run-down garage. Today, it's a super modern service station and convenience store.

As the hours passed, I nursed the one bottle of beer I'd agreed to take. It was past midnight and the whole scene was getting me down. There were two older guys who were not from the area. They showed up in an old camper with their guitars and wanted to make music around the fire. Tommy, who wanted to keep grooving to the driving beat, began calling them a bunch of old hippies. The guys did not seem very impressed by his macho redneck routine. They wished us good night saying they were going to head on down the beach.

"Great, get the hell out!" shouted our brave hero.

Karine, increasingly exasperated by Tommy, made a couple of comments that no one heard except the person for whom they were intended. He began to give her shit. It wasn't nice to see or hear. Everyone was uncomfortable. Chloé, who was sitting close to me, whispered that

I should go talk to him. I agreed ... more troubled by her hand on my arm than I was by Tommy acting like a jerk.

A whole evening basically ruined for everybody who had come to party at Pointe-Noire. Most just got up and left. Karine, who couldn't take her boyfriend a minute longer, disappeared into the night, probably to join the two older guys with the guitars.

"She can get the hell out too. Good riddance!" Tommy shouted, wiping his foam-speckled mouth on the sleeve of his team hockey jacket. "I'm getting the hell out of here myself!"

He looked at me through the flickering flames.

"Hey, boss. You coming?"

No way I'd be going anywhere with him. He was smashed out of his mind. The last time I found myself in a car with a drunk driver it was Mr. Pinchault's old Chrysler ... And I'd just as soon never think about how all that turned out. Don't worry about it, I told Tommy. I'd walk home. And that set him off even worse. He wanted to have it out with me right there, but I raised my hand and he calmed down immediately. Be reasonable I told him, and he took my advice.

He just wasn't the same person since Shawinigan drafted him. He was angry and belligerent, like he was being persecuted all the time. You couldn't tell him anything without him taking it the wrong way. He thought calling me boss was friendly, but it sounded plain stupid.

"Forget it," he said. "Makes no difference to me."

"Do you want to come fishing with me Sunday?" He nodded, his face red in the firelight.

We left each other with a handshake. I walked down the beach with Chloé and Anna-Maria. No one said a word, Tommy's behaviour had shocked us all. Before we had gone a hundred yards into the night we heard the noise of an engine starting. Then we saw the Comanche heading towards the 138. He hadn't listened to me. I should've stayed with him. I hoped he didn't break his neck.

I should have stayed with him like a real friend. But something else was happening that was even more compelling. Anna-Maria had headed off, and I accompanied Chloé home. Beside the house, under the fir trees, we kissed. She wasn't laughing any more. Now she was serious; it lasted more than an hour.

I didn't get much sleep. Tossing and turning under the covers, I couldn't stop thinking about her. We were on the beach, in the woods, halibut fishing in Stéphane Leblanc's boat, in Quebec City, straddling the ramparts with our feet dangling, looking at the old town together. All night long I imagined us in one scene after another, happy and in love. Finally I fell asleep in the early hours of the morning when my exhausted mind lapsed into peaceful slumber. But it didn't even last two hours. Because at 6 a.m., the alarm clock rang. Even though I'd barely slept a wink I was feeling great. I got dressed and washed up, with a couple of quick splashes of water to my face, and hit the road running for my morning jog.

The sun was up and shining. Birds were singing, and you could tell, despite the chill in the air, that it was going to be another hot day, just like yesterday. And today, my workout was going to be a cakewalk. I was going to lift weights, plant 1,500 trees and run barefoot on the sand at Pointe-Noire ten kilometres, no problem. In fact it would be Larry, in his big quad, who'd have a hard time keeping up with me.

I ran by Chloé's house. It wasn't on my usual run. I had to go through the village and then take RR2 and turn off on Cleary Rd. There were only a few houses there, spaced far apart, built on the side of a sandy hill dotted with stunted birch and spruce. Chloé lived in a relatively new house with her mother and grandmother. She had a brother and sister, both younger than her. She only saw her father twice a year in Quebec City, once over the holidays, and once over summer holidays. But this year, at the age of 16, she refused to go. She'd found a job in the garage owned by Mr. Escobar, Anna-Maria's father. And besides, she was going to college in the fall and would most likely be living with her father in Sainte-Foy. A terrifying thought, since she detested her stepmother. But that wouldn't be for long, she told herself, just until she could find her own apartment. She was going to look for some roommates. And since I was already planning to be in Quebec...

"I'm not sure I'm going to make the team," I said.

"I'm pretty sure you will."

I think that's when we kissed. Or maybe it was when she said she wanted to study art and began telling me about a log she had in her yard that she had sculpted with a chainsaw. Regardless, the fact remains that I finally wished her good night, and ran home through the woods in the dark, down a trail that led right to my house. I ran with my body thrust forward, head thrown back, moist warm breath steaming out of my nostrils. My antlers slashed through the crackling branches. Rooted deep in my head, they grew and grew as if lifting me up into the air. On I ran like a raging beast, leaving leaves and fir cones whirling behind me.

Needless to say, at 6:20 in the morning, everyone at Chloé's was still fast asleep. I ran by once, casting a glance at the side of the house near the trees, seeing us standing there in my mind's eye. Then I turned onto a path that brought me back to the 138. Once there, I caught my breath, running in place to unstiffen my ankles, then took off on the run towards Pointe-Noire.

There's not very much traffic on the road in the morning. Just a few trucks heading one way or the other. The civilized drivers move over to the middle, to avoid kicking up sand or rocks in my direction. Apart from that, I've got the road to myself. I can run on the asphalt for long stretches at a time without seeing a soul, without hearing anything except the sound of birds singing or the wind in the trees. It was at just such a moment that he hit me from behind.

I never heard him coming. Probably because I was focused on managing my efforts and maximizing my breathing to make sure my heart was getting all the oxygen it needed. His hand smacked into my sweat-soaked t-shirt, landing with full force between my shoulder blades. I was running at full speed and I lost my balance, veering to the right onto the gravel. Trying to slow my momentum, I twisted my right ankle, the same one that had sidelined me last season. I guess I've got bad karma when it comes to drunks.

My face grimacing in pain, I hopped up and down on my left foot. Tommy had stopped twenty metres away. He watched me as he skipped from foot to foot on the asphalt in his grey sweats, his hood curled over his head like a boxer.

"What the hell's the matter with you!" I yelled.

"You okay?"

Everything seemed all right. I shrugged and nodded. He kept hopping up and down, his massive thighs stretching his sweatpants. His shoulders were wide, his arms massive. He looked like a monster. I couldn't recognize him. It wasn't my friend I was looking at. It was the Terminator.

He didn't bother to apologize. When he saw that everything was all right, he took off on the run. I accepted his challenge, falling in behind him. Normally, I would have caught up with Tommy easily. I've always been faster than him. Plus, he'd put on weight with all his power workouts. I'd been working my aerobics since May; I was sure that I'd pull up beside him in no time. But it was just the opposite. I gave it everything I had; no way. He pulled away from me down the highway. There was no way I could catch him. Breathless, I stopped to watch as he kept his torrid pace, steaming ahead like a locomotive and disappearing down the next straightaway.

I stood there for a long time, stunned, staring at the empty road that snaked off into the distance. I crouched, hands resting on the black asphalt that was starting to warm in the morning sun. Off to my left, the sea was surprisingly calm, like a green mirror lit up by the rays of the sun rising over the horizon. I suddenly realized that not a single bird was chirping. Up and down the road, total silence. It was a curious atmosphere. I looked around me; the trees had fallen silent, feeding my impression that time had suddenly stopped still.

I was ready to turn back and head for home, when I spotted movement in the bushes further on down the road, just ahead of the curve where Tommy had disappeared. It had to be an animal. Probably a raccoon or a porcupine. But what appeared on the road stunned me. When I saw it come out of the weeds and step up onto the highway, I thought first of all it was a dog. But no dog looked anything like that. An animal that size couldn't be a coyote, either. With its long legs and muzzle, and its bushy tail trailing behind, I recognized what it was I was seeing for the first time in my life: a wolf.

He lifted his head as if trying to catch my scent in the air. I was getting nervous. I couldn't believe he was going to head towards me. These animals are usually shy. They don't attack humans. Still, when you find yourself face to face with this mythical beast that has for so long fed people's imaginations, it's impossible to keep your cool.

He seemed to size me up, as he would've done with prey. I thought about fleeing, but it was out of the question. I had to stand where I was, and show him I wasn't afraid of him. Still, maybe the animal was rabid or lost. Further on down the road I heard a truck downshifting.

Immediately, the wolf scooted across the highway and disappeared into the woods.

The truck flew by in a cloud of dust. Still sweaty, I shivered all over, despite the mounting heat. I could feel shooting pains in my ankle; I could barely put any weight on it.

◉

All day long I planted trees, doing everything I could to conceal my injury from my father. But later on, when I got to Pointe-Noire, I only took a few steps before Larry stopped me: he'd spotted my limp immediately. I stopped and looked out to sea. Long fleecy clouds were passing overhead, casting long shadows that darkened the surface of the green water. I took a deep breath, trying to let go of the anger rising up in me.

"What happened?" asked Larry.

"This morning, jogging. I lost my balance and twisted my ankle again."

"Let me see it."

I sat down on the ground and extended my ankle toward him. He looked it over, rotating my foot. He asked me to flex it a couple of times against the palm of his hand.

"It's not too swollen. That's good news. I'll take you to the hospital."

We spent the rest of the day and early evening at the hospital in Baie-Comeau. We wanted to see a particular doctor, a sports medicine specialist. He confirmed that it wasn't serious. But I needed a good week of rest before resuming training.

As we rolled down the road in his jeep, Larry mentioned that now I'd have plenty of time to sharpen my skates. I'd be back in action in time for the beginning of on-ice workouts. I agreed with everything he said while absolutely avoiding saying a word about what had really happened that day. If I'd said that Tommy had pushed me from behind, both Larry and my father would have gone nuts.

I hadn't forgotten to give him Sylvie's message, and Louis came in from the woods to pay the bills. Heavy silence prevailed at the dinner table, interrupted only by the clicking of knives and forks on plates and a few sighs from my father, which quickly sent his sister off the deep end.

"Louis, give it a break. Alex will be back in training in a week. Everything will work out."

My father excused himself and went to rinse his plate in the sink. Then he started cursing about the state of the roads and all the potholes. It was the Department of Transport's fault I'd gotten hurt. How many petitions had they signed up and down the Côte-Nord? It wouldn't change a thing. And all those poor car suspensions and athletes' ankles would have to go right on suffering for a long time to come.

"It's not just hockey," he added. "There's the tree planting. I need Alex if I'm going to finish on time."

"I'm planning to help out."

"No way. If you don't keep up with the gathering and your orders, you're going to lose customers. I'll have to hire someone."

My father picked up the telephone.

"Hello … Larry?"

So that's how Larry ended up spending the entire period of my convalescence planting trees in my stead. True enough, my father didn't leave him much of a choice. When he asked Larry to reimburse him for one week of the training program, my coach replied that it was impossible; he'd already spent the money on his quad.

"Well, good. I guess that means you'll have to show up for planting tomorrow morning."

Larry was proud to have said "yes" straight away. Even if he really didn't like being in the woods in the summer. In fact, he loathed the very idea of it. A day in the bush was his worst nightmare and from June to September he avoided it at all costs. He liked to fish but preferred the sea, where the wind blew steady.

What you should know is that Larry is a redhead with white skin, almost translucent. I—and even more my father—have the copper-coloured skin of the Innu of the Côte-Nord. As soon as Larry started planting, the black flies of the entire region decided to hold a meeting on him. They seemed to converge from miles around on the piece of fresh meat that was Larry. A pink and tender piece of meat you could bite off in large chunks. You could tell from one look at his face.

By the end of the first day, he'd turned not only completely red, roasted by the sun in spite of the sun screen he had slathered all over, but unrecognizable to boot: his face was swollen and bloated from fly bites.

The loyal soldier that had endured the quagmire of Bosnia and Herzegovina toughed it out for a couple more days. Then he never returned. His body swelled up from head to toe from all the bites. It was horrible. His fever shot up and an ambulance came to take him to the hospital.

My father, with the best intentions, sent him a bouquet of flowers to perk him up. But it seems Larry was allergic to them; it took an emergency injection to stop him from swelling up and suffocating.

Meanwhile, I had plenty of time to be with Chloé. We took long walks down the beach or in the woods. But we stayed out of sight, far from everyone. As if we wanted it to remain a secret. It seemed like a good idea. Gossip travels fast around here. And anyway, people would find out soon enough. The news was sure to get around quick. Which is mostly why we decided to keep it just to ourselves. Because around these parts when everyone knows you have a boyfriend or girlfriend, you might as well be married. You can't go anywhere without being asked how the other person's doing. So we kept quiet and tried to enjoy some privacy. We wanted to see if it was going to work out between us.

Plus, it's exciting to have a secret like that. I didn't feel like talking about it with Sylvie or my father. Not with Félix or Sam either.

"Where you off to?"

"Going for a walk."

"Alone?"

"Yeah."

And at every opportunity, whether in the shelter of a sand dune or beside a small hidden lake, we'd find ourselves locked in a passionate embrace that seemed to go on forever. We'd kiss until we had to go, and then, unable to break away, we'd go on kissing as though it was the last time we'd ever see each other.

Not bad.

Which is why, when Sunday came around, I didn't feel like going fishing with Tommy any more. I was angry with him. And it was as if my insistence in keeping the real circumstances of the accident to myself only intensified my anger. He would be to blame if my ankle healed badly, or not at all, and I failed to make the team. So there in the canoe, each time he cast his line in the water pretending as if nothing had happened, I felt like sending him overboard with a kick in the ass.

"So," he said, while trolling with his spinning reel, flicking his rod, "how much do you lift when you're bench-pressing?"

"I don't know," I said.

"What are you talking about, you don't know? You lift some weights and you've got no idea how much you're lifting?"

"I don't know, Tom. I couldn't care less."

He shook his head from left to right. He was about to say what a loser I was when his fishing pole arced and his reel started to spin.

"Yeah, baby!" he yelled.

He worked at exhausting his catch for a while with that almost sadistic satisfaction typical of sport fishermen. His incessant hollering echoed off the mountains.

I put the net in the water and Tommy deftly guided the fish into it. A magnificent speckled trout was wriggling in the net. Bigger than anything I'd ever seen: eighteen inches.

Tommy was beside himself with pride. He carried on like a football player who had just scored the winning touchdown. He lifted his hand high in the air to give me a high-five. I readied my hand without much conviction and he smacked me hard. He put everything into it, no doubt expecting a degree of resistance on my end, and his momentum carried him forward. The canoe began to tip and we almost capsized. As he landed in the bottom of the canoe on his butt, I tried to stabilize the craft as best as I could with outstretched arms.

"Man," he said. "What's with your little fairy high-five?"

And, flushed with success, he quickly baited his line. Without looking, he drew it back and cast with a sudden, awkward motion. The hook caught in my cheek, just below the eye. Before I could so much as holler, he yanked it back with all the strength of his great big arms.

Chapter 2

Sylvie patched me up. She insisted I go to the hospital to get stitches, but I refused. There was some adhesive tape in the first aid kit. I told her it would be okay.

"Adhesive tape! That's not going to hold like sutures. You'll have a nasty scar."

"That's no big deal."

I wanted to have a nasty scar on my face. Make me look mean. I knew it would have an effect on Chloé. And I was right. She gave me the whole serious injury treatment: pampering, little kisses, the whole kit. What a feeling.

That evening, Larry came by the house to see me and make sure I was doing the exercises he'd assigned me during my convalescence. He showed up in his usual pale blue jogging suit, wearing his smoky blue shades. Pink calamine to soothe his fly bites covered his face. Even though he was a lot better than before, he was still in a miserable state.

"Let me see," he said, coming up to me.

With a grimace, I tore off the bandage so he could take a look.

"We'll have to keep a close eye on it. If it doesn't improve, you'll end up disfigured."

I shrugged.

"How's it going with Tommy?"

"Not great. We don't see each other so much."

"Shit happens… Pretty soon you'll both be training together. I like Tommy a lot. He's a hard worker and he wants to succeed. But if I were you, I'd keep him always in my sights. Don't skate too long with your head down. Be sure you always know where he is on the ice. Because he's going to test you, you can count on it."

Could Tommy have been deliberately trying to hurt me over the past few days? I couldn't believe it. It had only been as a result of his clumsiness. Even if he'd turned himself into a hulk since he began pumping iron in his cousin's gym, I couldn't bring myself to believe he'd turned downright mean. Maybe we'd be competitors one day, but we'd always be friends, first and foremost. But after what Larry had said, I was a little bit concerned. I'd have to start watching out for him. And as for myself, once on the ice, I wasn't going to yield an inch. With my long reach and explosive speed, I was a force to be reckoned with and could dish it out to absolutely anyone.

Chloé's hair was tied up in a headband, with a long braid that hung down her back. She was wearing a black shirt splotched with paint, khaki camouflage pants with pockets all over and work boots. She was stocky, not too tall, with broad shoulders and hips and an irresistible pretty little face with a smile that never quit. She seemed designed to be happy, Chloé did. But now, for the first time since I'd known her, her smile was gone. And her eyes seemed to shine even brighter.

36

She grabbed the chainsaw at her feet, pulled firmly on the starter cord. The chainsaw started up on the first try, sending a cloud of blue smoke all over the yard.

Sitting on a lawn chair not too far away, I watched her work as I nibbled on vinegar chips and drank very lemony—and not very sweet—lemonade that Chloé's mother had made. It had my cheeks puckering. Chloé let out the clutch and the chain started to whirl, the engine singing at the top of its voice the song our forests knew so well.

She began to carve up a log, sending chips flying in every direction. She stopped only to brush the sawdust from her face or to spit out what had gotten in her mouth. After a while, looking not quite satisfied with herself, she turned off the saw and put it down.

I went over to where she was. And with both hands in my pockets, I looked at the carved-up log.

"What's it supposed to be?"

"Don't know."

It's true, you couldn't tell what it was.

"Not even a clue?"

"Not even one."

"You carve something and you don't have any idea what it is?"

"No idea."

We kissed each other like crazy.

I'd been dying to jump onto the ice since May. My ankle had healed. It was time. I've been playing hockey since I was old enough to put on skates. Some memories are fresh in my mind. I'm four years old, leaning on my little hockey stick to keep from falling. My father and some of his buddies are flying by on their skates as I turn circles. They make jokes and crack up laughing, hitting the ice with their sticks, calling to me to pass them the puck.

"Pass it to me, Alex!"

"To me!"

"No, to me!"

But without fail I feed the puck over to my father who heads for the net and scores. There's no feeling like it.

Hockey is so ingrained in my life that I start to go into withdrawal if I don't skate for a couple weeks. It's like the oxygen we breathe or the water we drink. If I don't skate for a while, I start to feel like I'm suffocating or dying of thirst. I'm like a junkie looking for a fix. In fact, I'm an addict. And Larry knows it.

That's why he was stringing me along; that's why he had me running barefoot in the sand, planting trees, and a whole bunch of stuff that wasn't relevant. He wanted me to work out and get in shape, but not play. What he actually wanted was for me to go into with-drawal. So when the time came to skate, it would be like food for a starving man, with all the passion of someone stranded for years on a desert island.

And it worked. As soon as I hit the rink, I felt like I had wings. My new blades bit into the ice with each thrust and then glided as I relaxed, then straightened my body. I was literally flying from one end of the rink to the other, jamming on the brakes and sending up a cloud of snow. I'd never felt this way before: so strong.

My confidence growing, I was convinced I was ready for anything: training, camp, making the team.

Tommy hadn't shown up yet. The story was that he needed a few days to finish his cousin's program. And it looked as though he could lift more than twice his own weight.

It was a kind of relief not to have to deal with him. I could work my ankle without any pressure. I skated for hours under the steely eye of Larry, who made sure I never settled into my comfort zone, and pushed me relentlessly to surpass myself: stop-and-go, weaving around cones, skating backwards. Which I did with genuine pleasure. Because it felt good having the ice to myself at the beginning of August. Which made Larry say I was a show-off and not a team player, that I should've been a figure skater. And in the evening, I would hook up with Chloé. We'd go stretch out on the beach, far from the bonfires, preferring the blackness of the night, the stars and the dark mass of the sea lapping at our feet.

The news broke two weeks before the start of training camp. Shawinigan and Quebec were involved in a trade. Two starters for a defenceman. A rookie rounded out the transaction: Tommy heard the news before me. He had a cell phone, and his agent was able to reach him immediately.

"Cool, eh?" he said before hanging up.

I listened to the message on the answering machine three or four times to make sure I had understood it. The second message was from Pierre, my agent. He confirmed the news and asked me to call him back to discuss a few details.

Settled in on the green couch like I was on an amusement park ride, I was perplexed: Was it a good thing or a bad thing? I couldn't figure it out. I called Chloé to tell her that we wouldn't be able to see each other that night.

My father came home from work around seven o'clock. It was raining, and he didn't usually like sleeping up at the camp on rainy nights. He was carrying two beautiful rainbow trout. Probably from the stock they'd seeded a few years earlier. He shook them in my direction, saying we were in for a real treat. Then, noticing the doubt on my face and that I seemed kind of down, he asked me what was going on. I told him.

"Good for you guys, that makes me happy," he said. "You're going to be able to help each other when things get tough. Nobody up there is going to be handing it to you on a platter. And especially not you, Alex, there's a couple of veterans gunning for you."

But seeing that I didn't exactly share his opinion, he started asking questions. And I had a hard time responding, unable to put my ideas in order. So I made up some nonsense that seemed to irritate him:

"Don't you think we'll be fighting for the same spot?"

He came to sit next to me, still holding his trout, dripping water onto the living room carpet.

"Alex, son, don't let that worry you. Tommy's just not in the same league as you. He'll be fighting for a spot on the fourth line. You belong on the number one line. You don't fight the same fights. Remember, we talked about it with Pierre. If you don't make the first or at least the second line, we're going to ask that you be sent back to the midgets."

With that, I sighed, shaking my head no from left to right. I couldn't stomach the idea that Tommy could make the team and that I might not.

"Alexandre, that's the way it is. You agreed back in the spring. It'd be useless for a talented guy like you to be banging it out on the fourth line at the age of sixteen. As for Tommy, it might be his only shot at the NHL. And I'm counting on you to be supportive. Got it?"

Supportive? That's a good one. My buddy is turning himself into some kind of a gorilla with his muscles growing at the same velocity as his brain is shrinking, and I'm supposed to be supportive. I hadn't told anybody that he'd knocked me down on the road the other day. It seemed to me that I had already done more than my share.

"Of course we'll work together," I said, not wanting to hurt my father's feelings. "We come from the same town."

"Great! Come on, let's get the trout going. Is Sylvie out?"

I followed him into the kitchen. The trout left a trail of blood on the floor. I went to get the mop and cleaned it all up while he was preparing the filets. Fish guts, fins and heads were lying on the kitchen table, stacked on a scrap of newspaper. I didn't know where Sylvie was. She could've been out in the woods or visiting friends. She didn't return until late in the evening. I was sleeping on the couch when she came in on tiptoe.

As she took off her shoes and coat, I got up and sleepily walked towards the stairs. As she brushed by me, I asked her where she had been. It wasn't her style to stay up late.

"None of your business, kid. You'd better hit the sack if you want to be able to get up tomorrow morning."

When Sylvie used that tone of voice on me, I knew she was hiding something. Usually something about a guy. I was sure of it. I didn't say anything, and went up to my room. I lay down on my bed knowing that wouldn't be the final word.

◉

She woke me up in the morning, shaking me vigorously by the shoulders. I opened my eyes, completely confused, as if I had been teleported back down to Earth on a space shuttle. How long had I been asleep? Sylvie was really upset. She threw my underwear and my socks on my bed and opened the curtains, tossing my dirty laundry to the back of the closet, doing everything all in a whirl like when I was little and about to miss the school bus. When she told me I was late for practice and that Larry had called, it was my turn to be really upset. It was Monday morning. It was a quarter past seven. The guys had already been skating for fifteen minutes and I wasn't there. I jumped out of bed.

All my gear was in the washing machine. I started the dryer while my father, who had also just gotten up, chewed me out, saying that from now on he'd have to come home and sleep at the house every night and that I was irresponsible. Sitting on the dryer, which was warming up my bum, I watched as he brushed his teeth, his broad back turned to me. I hadn't missed a single workout all summer, I told him. I'd gotten up every morning. He turned around with his mouth full of bubbles from the toothpaste, talking and spraying me with foam. I didn't understand a word, but I'm pretty sure he was telling me he didn't give a damn.

You can be sure that he spun the pickup's wheels coming out of the driveway, peppering the garage with gravel. Then we hightailed it into town like a couple of yahoos, right up to the arena. In the locker room, I was pulling on my still-damp gear, forty-five minutes late, when Larry came in. I started to apologize, but he simply raised his hand to silence me.

"I just got off the phone with your father."

"Larry…"

"Listen up. When I signed on to coach you, I met the both of you at the beginning of June. I said that you were going to have to do what I said and follow my recommendations. Otherwise, why go to all the trouble? Your father was in agreement, and you agreed too. We signed a contract, Alex. You have to respect it. Zero tolerance for lateness. Everyone's busted their ass to be on time. The guys are here to train, but also for the pleasure of playing with someone who's on his way to the juniors. You made the front pages of the papers in Quebec City when they held the draft. Do you get what I'm saying? It's not just me you'll be letting down. It's everybody. But the most important thing I want you to understand is that the biggest loser will be you. Are you with me? If you don't make the team, you'll be just another wet firecracker, like so many others."

I nodded that I'd had enough; that I understood. I knew perfectly well he'd gotten a kick out of giving my father an earful after what he'd suffered planting trees a few weeks back. As I walked out, he told me that if I was late one more time, he'd wind up the program. I could go find somewhere else to train. I didn't think it was true. He wouldn't let me down. He had even made arrangements to stay at his sister's in Quebec City so that he could be with me during camp and at the start of the season.

"Is Tommy here?" I asked, before Larry could close the locker room door.

"I'd say so. By the time everyone else showed up this morning, he had already been skating for over half an hour."

Half an hour, plus forty-five minutes… That added up to more than an hour he'd been training. And he never got tired.

Everyone greeted me with a nod, but no more than that. Not that they were angry at me for being late, like Larry claimed. The guys have known me for a long time. They knew it wasn't the first time I'd been late, and it certainly wouldn't be the last. None of them would've said a word about it. They were just too tired from the workout to say anything at all. On that Monday morning at the arena, Sergeant Larry had decided it was time for a gut check. He had piled it on, and they had given it all they had. They were drenched with sweat, gasping for breath. Everyone except Tommy, who seemed fresh as a daisy. On the other hand, even if his tongue wasn't hanging out like the others, he looked all pasty and puffed-up. Under the arena lights, you could see that there were pimples all over his face. Which I hadn't noticed before.

I skated circles alone in one corner of the rink, doing my warm-ups and then some power exercises. After he was sure that I was dead tired and had paid for my lack of discipline, Larry allowed me to join the others at the end of the rink for some technical exercises: passing and positioning. After that, we got to play for a while just to relax.

Bastien was in goal. Samuel and Félix were there. We played two on two. You had to come out of the defensive zone with the puck on your stick. Then you had to come in at top speed while the two opponents took up defensive positions. It was just a game, but as always, we competed full out.

Samuel and I paired up. Félix, small and fast, was with Tom. I noticed from the outset that Samuel seemed to be out of synch. Maybe he had something on his mind; maybe he wasn't quite in shape yet or maybe he just didn't have his heart in it. Most likely a combination of all three, but I was leaning more towards the idea that he had his mind on something else. He seemed like a guy who wasn't really enjoying himself, not because he didn't care, but more because he was feeling down, and because of his negative attitude. After every bad play, he'd criticize the other players or find fault with them instead of concentrating on improving his game. No doubt he wished he was still on vacation, having fun with his new girlfriend, sitting around the pool without a care in the world.

But Félix, he was totally involved. Always speedy and energetic, he covered me tightly, giving me no room to skate. I managed, with my long reach, to get enough space to make a pass. But, unfortunately, Samuel was no match for Tommy, who was making his life miserable. A linesman would've surely handed Tommy a couple of obstruction penalties for planting himself in front of Sam like a cement pillar. The poor guy was totally checked, incapable of budging Tommy so much as an inch. And since he was always quickly covered, I had no one to pass to. Despite making some good plays, we quickly fell behind, four to one.

I managed to score a second goal, but I had to do it by myself. I beat Félix with a nifty shoulder fake coming in on the left. I didn't even think about Samuel, figuring Tommy had him pinned to the boards. I came in alone against Bastien who did the splits. I lifted the puck and scored on my backhand. When Larry whistled the end of the game, we had lost, four to two.

Right at the end, I found myself along the boards battling Tommy for the puck. I was determined to beat him on my own, since Sam was so unconnected. I took a powerful shoulder check, as if I had run into a brick wall. I went down hard, unable to stay on my feet. Looking up, I saw Tommy give me a wink before leaving the zone with a strong thrust of his heavy blade.

"Okay, guys," said Larry, "that's it for today. Thanks for showing up on time. We took it easy today to set our pace. But I assure you, by the end of the week, you'll be wanting to call your moms to say you're finished with hockey. Tom, it's supposed to be no contact."

"But Alex hit me first."

Larry didn't respond, and I didn't protest, unable to take my eyes off Tommy's face. I couldn't believe he had

46

been so quick to squeal on me to the coach. A real friend would have kept it zipped. True, I'd given him a little action in the corner. But he'd been doing exactly the same from the get-go.

Tom, who might have had a secret lobotomy, looked at me with that stupid smile that never left his face. He was probably feeling pretty good about his first day on the ice and the amazing success of special training program his cousin from Baie-Comeau had put him through. It wasn't the hard fall that had me thinking— you have to expect things like that when you play hockey—it was mostly the fact that Tommy hadn't moved an inch that annoyed me.

That's how it was all week long! Tommy took to the ice, not fast, nothing fancy, but with thunderous form and extraordinary power. He was moving all the time, like a freight train, and no one was able to shove him off the rails. Every time he came to check me, I'd give ground, which put me on the defensive and made me vulnerable to his crushing hits. For the first few days, Larry insisted on no contact. But soon enough we started to play rough. You had to learn to be tough enough to take a hit from twenty-year-olds weighing over two hundred twenty pounds. At the beginning of our mini-camp, I went to the net like a bolt of lightning, scoring goals one after the other. My game was much better in every way than anyone else's, and no one seemed able to stop me. But soon, Larry made us tighten the game and play his man-to-man system, yielding as little space as possible, constantly back-checking. And slowly but surely, Tommy overshadowed everyone.

Claiming more and more space every day and becoming increasingly dominant. After six days, it was as if he owned the ice. And everyone trembled when they saw him coming. The boards trembled too, the glass whipping back and forth alarmingly and the thuds reverberating all over the rink whenever Tommy sent someone flying into them.

There were some new guys in camp. Gagnon and a talented young player, Nicolas Landry. Gagnon and I were the only ones who could stand up, if ever so slightly, to Tommy's intimidation. But Landry, who was only fourteen, went off to the locker room at the end of his second day, gasping for breath, his rib cage flattened, following an unfortunate encounter with our team bully, who had shown him no mercy. I didn't feel good about it when I saw Nic creamed into the boards.

Disgusted, I went to see Larry.

"Hey, tell him to calm down."

"Tell him yourself, he's your friend. So far, he's playing within the rules. It's up to the rest of you to handle it."

"He just about ripped Nicolas's head off!"

"Nic knew what he was in for when he decided to play with the older guys. He wanted it. He'll remember what he learned here when he's playing midget this year, and be a better player for it."

Really, now I'd heard everything. Larry could be a nice guy, but as soon as he set foot in a rink, it was as if he thought he was in a military barracks or a trench in Bosnia and Herzegovina. He became, like a soldier under enemy fire, a perfectly inhuman machine.

I wanted to respond, but he pointed his finger at me while looking me right in the eye, with his steely gaze, behind his smoky blue-tinted glasses.

"And you're going to have to toughen up, yourself. You can finesse everybody around here. You can talk a big game and fake everybody out. But it won't work like that in Quebec City. In a couple of years, you're going to be just like your father Louis: six four and over two hundred thirty pounds. You'll never be one of the fast guys in the NHL and you're going to have to learn to play more physically. I structured your training program with that in mind. You're a power forward, Alex, and don't you forget it."

I stood leaning on both elbows against the boards, watching my sergeant coach head towards his office. I felt a breath of cold air ripple along my back. It was Tommy, who always put in an extra half-hour skating after practice. He whizzed by me like a speeding loco-motive, practically melting the ice with every stroke of his skates.

"Are you sure?"

"Absolutely. What am I supposed to do with it in Quebec City?"

"But you'll be back over the holidays."

"Well in that case, I'll borrow it back."

Mike had just about stood on his head to turn down my offer to lend him the Skiroule. The snowmobile needed a good mechanic to keep it in top shape. My father had had his Polaris 500 fixed so he wasn't likely to be puttering along at 30 clicks an hour in my semi-antique. I didn't want it spending the winter hibernating in the back of the garage either. It was like a living thing. I'd seen the proof plenty of times last winter; she needed to move, to slide along the snow, to be treated with care. But the main thing was that Mike still had bad memories of what happened up at Lake Matamek, when I forced him to throw his Leafs hat at my feet. He didn't like thinking about his long ordeal and the humiliation that went with it. He knew I absolutely couldn't tolerate him wearing a Bruins cap. He must have smelled the trap.

"Why don't you leave it with your girlfriend? She'd have fun with it for sure."

I pretended not to know what he was talking about and he started cracking up.

"Sorry, sonny boy. But you must be the only one in town who thinks you don't have a girlfriend."

So that was that. The cat was out of the bag. I was seeing Chloé. Everyone knew it. We might as well call the priest and set the date. A wedding between two villagers. That would make everybody happy. Great for the local gene pool too. And I looked down to see if someone hadn't strapped ten pounds of lead to my feet. This time, if I jumped into the water, there'd be no one to save me. Not even Mike. I'd sink straight to the bottom.

Mike tossed his wrench onto the workbench. He tapped me on the shoulder and then we went for a walk on the dock.

It was mid-afternoon and there were quite a few fishermen there. The Boivin brothers, two retired gentlemen, would spend almost every day fishing for smelt, mackerel and flounder. The whole town would gather there on a summer's evening. That's why every rumour had the same source: the dock. Old folks and young: people of all ages mixed together. Some were listening to music and drinking beer. Others indulged in their favourite pastime. The fishing was good when the east wind was blowing and the tide high, and the village fishermen thoroughly enjoyed themselves. Smelt and mackerel lay scattered on the dock, flopping back and forth on the asphalt.

Mike and I worked our way through the crowd of people, greeting everyone we knew. Some of the guys offered us their rods, inviting us to take advantage of the great fishing, but we turned them down, continuing on our way out to the lighthouse. The government had built a security fence just in front of it, since the old dock was showing signs of wear. We climbed over it and clambered down to the pier.

Seated comfortably in between the large rocks piled up to reinforce the original concrete structure, we stayed there for a long time, silently looking out to sea. A long swell rolled in, a sure sign that a storm was on the way. When the waves come in from the east, you can usually predict a low-pressure system will follow, bringing with it a couple of days of bad weather. The waves usually come before the wind and the clouds. Judging by the size of them, we knew that we were in for a whale of a storm.

Long waves that had started in the faraway gulf were gently ending their journey against the rocks.

"I've started going out with Sylvie," said Mike, stretching his legs.

"I know," I said.

…Even if it wasn't exactly true. But at least I found out why she came in late the other night, and that made me happy. It more than made up for sleeping in and being late for hockey practice.

A longer, taller wave than the others curled over the ebbing surf and crashed heavily onto the jetty, sending spray high into the air. In no time at all we were completely soaked. In the warm sun still shining through the clouds, it was a great feeling.

It was probably Chloé's and my last chance to be together, at least for a stretch of time. Sure Sylvie had invited her for dinner the night before I left, but we decided we'd rather be alone since I'd be in Quebec City and on the road throughout the fall and winter. We weren't going to have much of a chance to see each other. I took Michel's advice and offered her the Skiroule.

Sitting side-by-side on the stairs, only the sound of passing trucks interrupted our heart-to-heart talk.

When I asked her if she wanted the snowmobile, she started to giggle.

"Thanks, but no thanks. I don't know how to drive those things."

"It's not that complicated."

Side by side we walked to the garage. When I pulled the dusty cover from the 1970 Skiroule 440 I noticed the change come over her. She stopped laughing and went over to the machine, eyes wide. Chloé was an artist and I just knew she was going to love my old vintage skidoo. I showed her how to start it, giving the pull start a yank.

Chloé shook her head from side to side, laughing. She must have been imagining her mother and grandmother's faces when they saw her sliding along, come winter.

Already the two biddies, who took tea every afternoon at four o'clock sharp, had enough trouble with the fact that she was out in the yard running a chain saw; when they saw their little Chloé flying around at top speed on a skidoo they would be sure to faint dead away. No way they were going to accept the idea. For sure that was what Chloé had in mind when she enthusiastically accepted my offer as she sat on the shiny leather seat, gunning the motor and making faces. Choking on the fumes we rushed out to the garage, buzzed and sick to our stomachs, but having a lot of fun.

My father finally arrived around five o'clock in the evening. I recognized my quad's distinctive sound. Like a show-off, he swerved into the driveway sending dust flying every which way. It was to be his first meeting with my first—official—girlfriend and he was trying to be funny. I thought for a moment he was going to go straight through the yard, jump the fence on top of the rise and finally land in the sandpit. But he got control of the Suzuki just in time. Then, feeling proud of himself, he pulled up in front of us, one knee poised on the seat.

He took off his bright orange hat and shook the long grey hair that he wore Indian style, like in a shampoo commercial. He was quite a sight, his shirt unbuttoned to the navel, and even worse, that big forced smile of his.

"Hi Chloé," he went.

"Hello, Mr. McKenzie."

"Mister's for my father. I'm Louis."

I hate that reply. Can't stand it: "Mister's for my father." Blah blah blah. I was seriously ticked off.

Chloé laughed and so did my father, turning on the charm and running his fingers through his hair. Then he began to tell us about his day's work: the desiccated trees provided by the government; the inspector who was supposed to come the week before and still hadn't shown up; Jean St-Pierre who had come to give him a hand. It wasn't so much the empty chatter that was getting on my nerves, no, it was the way he pulled his hair over his shoulder and began nonchalantly to braid it matter-of-factly. Of course, it attracted Chloé's attention, and she began asking him questions. Then they started comparing each other's hair and braiding techniques. I wasn't feeling great.

As she leaned closer to him the better to observe his hair, he gave me the thumbs up sign to let me know I'd snagged myself a fine filly. Me, I let him know I wasn't amused.

"What's the matter, son?"

"We've been waiting for you for two hours."

"Sorry. I had to make a stop up at Robert Pinchault's. He wanted to show me the inside of the barn now that it's finished. You ought to go see it. He asked after you."

Sylvie, always perceptive, had been watching her brother's performance through the window. She hurried out to tell him she needed his help right away. The tap was leaking in the upstairs bathroom and she was afraid there would be water damage. I knew she was lying, and I made a mental note to remember to thank her. By the time my father realized that Sylvie was playing a trick on him, we were deep into the forest.

Chloé hugged me hard from behind while I accelerated up Mill Road. We were heading up to the cabin where we would spend the night.

The sun was setting behind the mountain, but we still had two hours of daylight left. We dropped our packs off on the porch and went down to the water's edge. I pushed the old canoe into the water and we made for the middle of the lake, Chloé paddling awkwardly in the front, and me steering in the back. A loon cried off in the distance, warbling its long, sad song. The still water of early evening reflected the clouds as they turned blue edged with orange in the fading light.

There we cast our lines, letting them sink down deep to the bottom. I wanted to impress Chloé, and I knew we could find some spectacular trout there. All of a sudden I felt water around my knees. I hadn't noticed any leaks the last time I'd gone fishing with Tommy. It struck me as curious. After having twisted my ankle and almost ripped out my eye, could he have possibly punched a hole in my canoe to drown me? It didn't make any sense.

My first thought was to go ashore near the beaver dam, but the water is low at this time of year. Branches you can't see in the spring, gnawed to a sharp point by the beavers, make an impenetrable barrier to any approach in the shallow water. I could have tried walking on the bottom, but I would have sunk deep into the mud, which didn't seem like a great idea. So I concluded the best thing would be to turn back, even if I wasn't sure we'd make it. The canoe was filling up fast.

Chloé, seeing the water rising in the canoe, was getting nervous.

"Don't worry," I said. "Everything's under control. We'll get back in time."

Whatever... By the time we found ourselves out in the middle of the lake, I was seriously beginning to wonder if we were going to make it. We might have to swim. We'd be able to do that without any problem. I was pissed at myself, remembering that I'd seen the bailing bucket in the thicket at the edge of the water, and didn't bother to bring it along. Which might mean that I risked losing all my fishing gear.

I was heavier than Chloé. And the canoe's stern was sinking deeper and deeper. Every stroke of the paddle was tougher than the one before, and it was getting harder to keep the canoe level. Even though nobody could see us, we pretended that nothing was wrong. We reached the flat rock in front of the cabin just in the nick of time. Water completely covered the stern and was pouring in over both sides.

It was no easy task to turn the canoe over and empty the water. When I finished, and set the canoe on a couple of birch logs, and then I inspected the wicked little hole that must have been punched out by I don't know what, I turned to find Chloé … half naked. She'd taken off her jeans and t-shirt and stood watching me, wearing only her bra and panties. She was shaking like a leaf.

I froze, dumbfounded, looking her up and down. She was short and plump and her long wet black hair hung down over her shoulders and back. Her belly stuck out a bit, and she had broad hips, and heavy breasts that her bra could barely contain. The girl who was always comfortable anywhere and with anybody, now for the first time seemed bashful and uncertain. Maybe she didn't like the shape of her body. Me, I thought she was very pretty, but I think it was mostly my inquisitive and clumsy eye that made her feel ill at ease. I didn't know what to say, but I knew what I should do. I went over to her, hugged her against me, and she stopped shivering. We stayed for a long time in each other's arms, stretched out on the big rock still warm from the heat of the day. When the last rays of sunlight had disappeared and all you could see were the stars, we walked barefoot to the cabin. Chloé was shivering again. Her lips were blue. I lit a fire in the stove while she began making dinner. Once the fire was crackling, I went outside to get some wood from the woodpile.

It was a clear night with no moon. The stars above my head were dizzying. If you stared at them long enough you felt like you could fall right into the Milky Way. I called out to Chloé.

"Close the door, there's too much light!" I told her.

When she joined me, I pointed up to the sky. She looked up. After a few seconds of holding her head all the way back, she began to sway. I put my arm around her waist to support her.

"I almost fell!" she exclaimed.

Our eyes were burning for one another. We were about to join in a passionate kiss when from far away, a long howl rang out over the lake and the forest.

"Is this the first time you've ever heard one?" I asked.

"Yes," she replied. "I think so."

It was a wolf. A moment later, the pack responded in full chorus to the call of what appeared to be a lone animal.

As usual, I hid my emotions, a reassuring smile on my face. But even if it didn't show, I was feeling uncomfortable. And maybe a bit nervous.

I'd heard wolves howling before, during trips deep into the woods with my father. Louis would tell me about them with a passion. He came alive, as if captivated by magic. With shining eyes, he would try to locate them. According to my father, who felt completely at home in the woods, the little boy who was his son had no reason ever to be afraid. He could have vanquished a black bear in hand-to-hand combat and it wouldn't have surprised me. Now, it was my turn to provide a measure of comfort and reassurance. I felt unsure of myself. Would I be up to the task? I knew full well that there was absolutely no danger. The wolves would never come close to the cabin, and there was no way they'd ever attack us. Even so, my encounter with the strange creature on the road a few days back had left me feeling less certain. The howling of a wolf pack in the northern forest is always something fascinating and disturbing.

Chloé headed back up to the cabin to finish cooking dinner, while I adjusted my headlamp and headed out behind the cabin where we stacked the firewood. The beam of light swung from side to side, lighting the path in time to my steps. The wood was stored in a little shelter about twenty metres away. My father had spent a lot of time up at the cabin over the summer because of the transplanting project. The stack was getting low and there was hardly any birch, mostly softwood, and pretty green at that. While shining my lamp here and there in hopes of finding another cord that might have been stacked further away, my eye was drawn to the top of a low hill. There was something up there that looked like a pile of rocks. Intrigued by the unfamiliar pile, I climbed up to the crest, using the trunks of the small evergreens that grew on the flanks of the hill as handholds. There I found a pile of rocks in the shape of a person. It was a small inukshuk, a symbol the Inuit use to mark their trails through the huge expanse of semidesert land in the Far North.

It was hard for me to imagine my father building an inukshuk in the woods just to amuse himself. It wasn't his style and it didn't make any sense. When I saw the dug-up earth and the traces of fur and bone, I immediately thought of the grave of Nuliak, Mike's dog. I remembered when he asked me if he could bury him on our land last winter. I never would have thought he would bury her within fifty feet of the cabin. It had been well into December when he dug up the frozen ground.

Unfortunately the hole wasn't deep enough, and scavengers had dug up the carcass for food. I could see the bones with darkened flesh still sticking to them scattered around; maggots were crawling over them. It made me sick. I had to step back for a moment and take a few deep breaths. Once my disgust had passed, I gathered everything I could find by the light of my lamp. With the old rusty shovel that I found under the cabin, I began to dig a "real" hole to bury the old husky's remains.

I hadn't turned over three shovelfuls of earth when I once again heard the howl of the wolf. I stood completely still and pricked up my ears. My father had taught me that wolves could fool you; that it was hard to tell where their howl was coming from. You think the wolf is in a particular place when it's actually somewhere else. And with the echoes bouncing off the lake and the mountain, I couldn't tell where the howl was coming from. But one thing was for sure; it was closer now. And while I was thinking about that, I heard the pack respond far off in the distance.

I started digging again when I heard the cabin door open, with a distinct creak of its hinges. They needed oiling; it was spooky. Down the hill, I could see a beam of light shining from the porch to the lake. I heard Chloé calling me.

"What are you doing?"

"I'll just be a minute. Some animals have made a big mess up here."

She said something I couldn't hear as I had just struck a rock with my shovel. I yelled for her to repeat what she had said. But this time, she didn't hear me, since she had closed the cabin door behind her. It was a big rock and even using the shovel as a lever, I couldn't lift it. I got down on my knees and grabbing it with both hands I managed to turn it over with a great deal of effort.

It was then that I felt a blinding pain in my left knee. I cried out, falling on my side holding my leg with both hands. A sliver of bone had pierced my jeans and lodged in my kneecap. Fortunately, it hadn't gone in too deep and I was able to pull it out without causing any bleeding.

But when I stood up I could barely put any weight on my leg. By the light of my headlamp, I realized I'd been kneeling right on a pile of bones and decomposing flesh and that I'd rolled right in it when I had fallen. I finished the job, burying the remains. With a sense of satisfaction, I tamped down the soil with the back of my shovel, promising myself that I'd give Mike a piece of my mind first chance I got.

With my shovel on my shoulder, I was just about ready to leave when I suddenly shivered and my blood froze. I was certain there was someone or something behind me, watching me. All my senses were on full alert. I could hear the breeze ruffling the leaves. The rustling of the brook and the lapping of the lake water against the shore. It was too dark to see anything. But there was no mistaking the odour on the air. It was musky and definitely alive. My heart was pounding in my chest and my pulse was racing. I wanted to take off running, but I knew I mustn't panic. I had to stay cool. A northwest wind was blowing. The smell had to be coming from there. With an impulse that I can't explain, I turned off my headlamp, as if I had suddenly realized my life was in danger and that it would be a good thing to disappear. As if the darkness would be my friend if I had to flee.

Fear held me in its thrall. Slowly my eyes adjusted to the dark and I turned around. The treetops were outlined against the sky. Before me stretched the spruce forest, black and opaque. I couldn't make out a thing. Yet I was sure something was watching me. Something was out there, crouching in the dark. I could feel its anxiety, its desire ... Its hunger.

As my eyes played over the nocturnal forest, I saw the flicker of two incandescent flames: the eyes of the wolf. I was spellbound. It was as if the entire forest was converging from all directions toward this intense gaze.

I took a long, deep breath, inhaling to fill my lungs with oxygen. My heart was pounding too, pumping blood into my muscles; I could feel them warming. And my senses were on a razor's edge, alert to the slightest movement or sound, the faintest odour. Then, suddenly, he sprang at me. I bolted, running with all my strength, leaping from the crest of the hill, carried along by my momentum. I spotted the lake and the cabin, then tumbled violently to the ground a few metres along. I sprang back onto my feet and kept going. I took the cabin steps four at a time and burst in with a bang, slamming the door behind me.

Busting in like a fugitive from an insane asylum, I frightened Chloé half to death; she screamed. She was standing there in front of the table, arms crossed, eyes and mouth wide open, wide-eyed. It took her a couple of tries before she could get it out:

"My God, Alex, what happened?"

"Nothing."

"Nothing?"

She shook her head from side to side as though she was dealing with the biggest weirdo in the world.

I didn't want to tell her that I'd seen the wolf. That he was still out there, behind the cabin, that he was definitely watching us. Most of all, I didn't want to let on that I was scared shitless. So I smiled the dumbest smile I could, my thumbs hooked into my pockets. Seeing her sit down, a puzzled look on her face, I wanted to go over to her, but she raised her hand to stop me. It wasn't the howling of the pack that frightened her; it was me. I was filthy. When I fell to the ground after hurting my knee, I rolled over Nuliak's remains, tufts of husky fur clung to my hunting jacket and jeans. With my bewildered and frightened expression, I wasn't exactly going to be winning any beauty contest.

"Umm," I said, dusting off the fur stuck to my clothes, "there was a dead animal lying around out back. I had to dig it a proper grave. The scavengers won't be bothering it anymore. I promise."

And I laughed out loud, while she kept silent, her face impassive.

We ate our spaghetti without a word. Chloé's mom's sauce wasn't as good as my aunt Sylvie's. But it seemed better not to mention it.

The rest of the evening we spent in almost total stillness. Every time I tried to get close to her, she moved away. And when I finally took her in my arms, I could feel that she was embarrassed and uncomfortable, trading kisses but not really putting her heart into it.

Odours are important. Even if we don't always realize it. And me, that night, I stank. I stank of carrion: of dead dog.

So I didn't say a thing. Or do anything all evening. I wasn't really there with her. We were a hundred thousand kilometres apart. Each of us alone with our thoughts. My mind and my sharpened senses were concentrated outdoors, listening for the sound of footfalls and trying to catch the animal's scent. Throughout the night I got up to stoke the stove. She lay wrapped in her sleeping bag, back to me and face to the cabin wall. She wasn't asleep and I knew it. When daylight came, I was relieved that the night was over. I think I slept for an hour or two, around five or six in the morning. When I got up, Chloé was already dressed and ready to go. She had to get back, no time for breakfast, she had too much to do. That night, as planned, she came over for dinner. My father put on his clown act and Sylvie tried to lighten the atmosphere by being as nice as possible to Chloé, who, in her easygoing way, jumped right into the conversation, showing interest in everything: my aunt's salty herbs and my father's stupid jokes. But I could see that she was worn out. Our evening together had taken a lot out of her. After dessert, Louis and Sylvie pretended they were tired and went off to bed, at nine o'clock. They wanted us to have the living room and the sofa to ourselves. No sooner had they disappeared upstairs than Chloé told me she was too tired and asked me to drive her home. Which I did without a peep.

We traded cold and lifeless kisses. She walked hesitantly towards her house, and then turned about and ran up to me. Then told me she loved me. But I didn't believe it. I just nodded, like a jerk, unable to respond. A confused look glazed her eyes and she vanished behind the front door.

I gunned the quad and popped a wicked wheelie that carried me all the way down the street. I hopped the ditch, and headed full-speed down the trail that leads to the 138. I exited the bush six feet in the air, trailing dead leaves, grass and pine branches behind me and landed in the middle of the highway, in front of a van that had to jam on the brakes, leaving rubber on the road. The driver, infuriated, blasted the horn a couple of times with a sound that echoed off the mountains. But with the throttle cranked to the max, I was already far away, headed straight for the beach.

Fires were twinkling along the shore. There were a lot of people out, partying. I kept on rolling like a demon, hopping dune after dune, as if each time I hoped to rise up flying toward the stars. No such luck. It wasn't just my heart that was heavy, but the Suzuki too, and we always fell back to earth, landing hard. The shocks hit bottom and the frame rattled with every blow, which I absorbed, swearing. I imagined that the people sitting around the fires were wondering who the idiot was that had just roared by at such an ungodly hour and in such a peaceful place. Well, it was me.

Later on, sitting alone on the sand, I looked out towards the dark sea. The tide was out and the smell of the seaweed and jetsam tingled my nostrils, and then straight into my heart. From time to time, I spotted a bird picking its way through the tidal pools that seemed like giant mirrors laid out on the ground. It was a shore-bird, making the best of low tide to search through the mud for crabs and other tiny shellfish. Suddenly I knew it was time to get out. There was nothing more for me to say, nothing more for me to do. I turned my back to the sea and drove home. The next day my father and I were speeding down the 138, next stop: Quebec City.

Chapter 3

We drove around for a good half-hour before we finally found a parking place. My father was tense; you could see how he hated the city. Nothing could have stopped him from being there for my first day of rookie camp, but it was just as clear he'd be hitting the road as soon as he had fulfilled his fatherly duty, and I wasn't about to blame him. He gets pretty itchy when he hears the call of the wild. And the call of the backwoods trails of the Côte-Nord would have been getting louder the longer we circled around and around the narrow streets of Quebec City's Saint-Roch district.

I didn't have a clue about the place. Never even heard of it before. But I quickly learned it was a strange place to live, in the opinion of people who didn't live there, of course. Whenever I walked down the street, I felt like I was on another planet. A feeling that grew stronger every time I mentioned where I lived, whether to someone on the staff or to reporters who were interviewing me. They were expecting to hear something like Lac-Beauport, Charlesbourg or Sainte-Foy. I'd stopped counting the raised eyebrows and know-it-all smiles.

"If you're looking for another place, don't hesitate to ask me," said an assistant coach, as if I had just told him that I was going to live in a trash can for the coming year.

Whenever I ran into a negative reaction towards the neighbourhood I lived in, I'd shrug my shoulders and explain that I liked it just fine where I was. Because it didn't take long before I started to notice the similarities between a typical Côte-Nord town and places like Saint-Roch, Saint-Sauveur and Limoilou, with their down-to-earth residents, so very much more real than what you'd find in the boring and standardized suburban dormitory communities.

Larry's sister Nathalie owned a duplex on Rue du Roi. She lived upstairs with her two children, and agreed to rent the downstairs flat to her brother. That's where we'd be living for the next three years, providing Tommy and I could get along, that is.

Larry had seen my father's pickup driving by; he was waiting on the sidewalk with a beer in his hand dressed in his imperishable blue jogging pants and a white tank top that showed his shoulders, which still bore the scars of his adventure in the woods: sunburn and mosquito bites.

"Hi guys!" he said.

Even though he was born on the Côte-Nord, Larry sticks to himself; nobody knows much about his personal life. He was born in Forestville. His father died when he was a teenager and his mother, who has Alzheimer's, lives in a nearby nursing home. Maybe that's why I almost didn't recognize him. For someone who has so much character, who is so rebellious, he appeared smaller than his usual self. As if he had shrunk. You got the feeling that he was embarrassed to have to introduce some members of his family to us. Maybe we would learn some kind of terrible secret. But to be frank, everyone knows there's something odd about Larry. So nothing was likely to surprise us.

Walking down the sidewalk littered with sand and cigarette butts, my father began to rail against the city, saying how much he hated it and how he couldn't believe that anyone could actually live there. While he was ranting, I trailed behind him, lugging my hockey bag and my suitcase. The heat was scorching. The asphalt was burning hot and I was drenched in sweat. Larry, who pretended not to be listening to Louis, grabbed my duffle bag and we entered a small five and a half.

The front door opened onto the living room. There was a small sofa covered in light brown corduroy, a wooden table and a TV. Past the living room was a large bedroom, which was where Larry would be sleeping. We then moved to the kitchen, which was rather large, with a small table and four folding chairs. Through the kitchen were two other small bedrooms, which were going to be Tommy's and mine. The bathroom was all the way in the back. Another door opened onto a small porch and a grassy yard, enclosed by a fence whose brown paint was peeling off. In her little garden, we found Nathalie on all fours, weeding. She had red hair like her brother. She was taller than him, something that surprised me. She had the same small bloodshot eyes, icy blue, that put you ill at ease when they sternly came to rest on you. And thanks to which, even if you hadn't done anything wrong, you'd begin to wonder what you'd done wrong.

"So, you're the one everyone's calling Quebec City's new saviour."

She said it in an unfriendly, maybe even contemptuous way that made me dislike her immediately. I shrugged my shoulders. I wasn't looking to be anybody's saviour or child prodigy. But I was going to have to learn to live with it. Over the coming days, I'd quickly learn that things work differently in the big city than in small towns. Back home, I knew absolutely everybody. People there genuinely like each other and everyone takes pride in each other's achievements. In the city, the proximity and the distance both lead to ways of relating with others that can be surprising and not even very human. Fame can arrive in a flash, and it can be overwhelming, like a crazy tidal wave that picks you up and carries you away and there's nothing you can do about it. But it can also be a double-edged sword, which can turn against you and suddenly plunge deep into your heart. That would turn out to be the greatest benefit of living in this curious little community, where people have been just what they appear to be for a very long time. It's no place to be putting on airs. Only by being sincere can you stay out of the quicksand and keep on moving forward.

My bedroom looked out over the yard. I sat down on the single bed and bounced up and down to test its hardness. The springs creaked.

And the pillow, with its synthetic stuffing, wasn't at all comfortable. Still, the room was clean enough, except for the basement smell coming from the hot water radiator under the window. My father leaned into the room, his arms resting on the top of the door frame, and watched me settle in. The entire wall creaked under the weight of his two hundred and fifty pounds.

"Don't worry," he said, "you won't be living here forever. Just while you're in Quebec City."

Yep, I said to myself. And sat down on my bed and, through the window, watched Nathalie's two children, aged seven and ten, down in the yard yelling and throwing handfuls of sand in each other's faces. The boy, named Michael, had tried to make his little sister Elisa eat cat shit, and Larry's sister was bawling him out. Larry was no slouch as a yeller himself. You could tell where the two children and their mother had gotten it from. What more proof did I need of the blood ties connecting my sergeant coach to these folks?

I went shopping with my father at the mall in Sainte-Foy to buy all the stuff we couldn't find back home. Sylvie had drawn up a long list. Larry spent his time trying on sunglasses, but he ultimately put them all back on the display rack saying he couldn't make up his mind. I kept telling him that this or that pair suited him perfectly. But, firmly and with conviction, he resisted, relying on his trusty smoky blues to define his look and his attitude. Missed opportunity.

Our little outing ended with a big surprise that really picked me up. My father bought me a laptop; a brand new PC. It would replace the prehistoric old clunker we had at home. And it would keep me busy during the sure-to-be long nights I'd be spending in my coach's sister's tiny apartment.

Later on in the evening, just like that, my father hit the road. He had to get out of town, in a hurry.

"At this hour?"

"Yeah."

"You're going to drive all night?"

"I'm going to stop in Les Escoumins and sleep at my cousin's."

"You're going to show up at one in the morning?"

He didn't answer me. In any case, he was just saying the first thing that came into his mind. If he got too tired he'd pull over at a rest stop and sleep in the truck. Or whatever; he just had to get going. A couple of times while shopping I completely lost sight of him, then found him in Sears—or was it The Bay?—hiding between two racks of clothing, like a trapped animal, cornered. And, like he was a child, I told him to come along, we weren't going to spend all day waiting. It always took everything he had to hold on to the little bit of calm he'd carved out for himself. He merged into the crowd at Place Laurier, walking with his back straight and his arms stiff, like a stone golem, eyes wide like a hunted deer caught in the open. I'd never seen him act that way in a crowd. It was then that I realized that my father was afraid of crowds.

So he left in a hurry, without so much as a goodbye.

Larry and I set up a training program. I had to keep in shape. It was Friday and camp would start Monday. I couldn't afford three days off. I had to show up warmed up and ready to go. I had to be hot, hot, hot, like a race-car engine. So the coaching team would have eyes only for me.

"It's just like love. The first impression is always the best."

I looked at Larry sceptically. If he was right, my chances of success seemed mighty slim. Because from the time I was old enough to be interested in girls to the present moment, my luck was zilch. No doubt I'd be sent packing with a kick in the butt. I could already see the headlines in the sports section: "Top Côte-Nord Prospect Sent Home." Or, "Not this Year for Alexandre McKenzie."

Next morning I headed out for my first training run through Quebec's Basse-Ville. I quickly discovered a pleasant-enough route that hugged the St. Charles River. It helped me find my bearings in an urban landscape that I would never really feel at ease in. The river and the ducks in Cartier-Brébeuf Park would help me keep my sanity. But just barely. I'd always miss the wide-open spaces, the forest and the sea.

Larry decided to join me on what he called his "Shape Up Fitness Program." The paunch he'd developed wasn't exactly disappearing. Too much sitting up on his Grizzly I kept on telling him. We ran side by side for a while until we reached Victoria Park. It wasn't long before his tongue was hanging out. His sweat-covered face was flushed. At 6:30 a.m., it was already hot. I had a lot, and I mean a lot, of fun watching him struggle. I could easily have spent the entire day pushing him harder and harder, knowing he was too proud to quit. Unable to take so much as one more step, he'd have collapsed on the asphalt right on his face with a twisted ankle or a dislocated shoulder. He'd have looked up at me in pain, helpless, his face all scratched up and covered in dirt. But I had to stick to my training schedule. I had to be in top shape, ready to succeed. And I had precious little time to waste.

"Sorry, Larry, but you're holding me back."

"Go on, go on!" he said, barely understandable through his gasping and wheezing.

I looked at him up and down, then asked him if he was going to be okay. Too proud, as usual, he nodded for me to go on without him; I picked up the pace. Two blocks further and he was out of sight. On freshly cut grass, I flew past the giant trees growing in the park one after the next.

It was a pretty good run. But not as good as it should have been. Larry said it was normal; on account of pollution. In the afternoon, I went out to the yard to play with Michael. He played goalie while I shot tennis balls at him with a street hockey stick. I could hear Nathalie's phone ringing on the top floor. She came out on the balcony yelling my name at the top of her voice. I took the stairs four at a time and she handed me her portable. I moved as far away from her as I could and covered my ear with my hand; she was ranting and swearing at Larry for not having a line installed, she wasn't going to be everybody's secretary. As soon as I got back to my own apartment, I sat on the sofa in the little living room to talk with Monique, my agent Pierre Anctil's secretary.

"*Le Soleil* wants to interview you Monday, after practice."

"Umm, I don't know."

"What do you mean you don't know? Pierre thinks it's a great idea."

The doorbell rang. With the phone tucked between my ear and my shoulder, I opened the door and found myself face to face on the landing with a large and muscular man. He was a head taller than me, with close-cropped hair and a tanned face. I told Monique I'd meet the journalist at the Colisée after practice, then hung up the phone, my eyes fixed on Mr. Muscles. His jaw was angular and massive. He had blond hair, streaked with grey and tied in a ridiculous little pony-tail combined with a sharply receding hairline. The guy must have been at least fifty. He spoke quickly, sniffing constantly. His clenched jaws made him mumble so badly I had to pay close attention.

"Huh?"

"Is Tommy Courchesne around?"

He had a high-pitched voice, in a stark contrast to his heavy-set and muscular build.

"Uh … no," I said. "He'll be arriving tomorrow."

"Good … Tell him Vincent, his cousin's friend, came by. Tell him to call me. Vincent's my name. Vincent."

"Okay."

He handed me his card. On it was printed the name Vincent Fradette with the title of Professional Trainer and the name of a gym in the Basse-Ville. I watched as he turned and left without so much as a goodbye. He crossed the street and got into a slightly rusted white Nissan Maxima with tinted windows. I could see the driver through the open window, an unfriendly looking guy with a red, white and blue scarf on his head and a big black beard. He threw me a glance in passing as I closed the front door behind me.

When I went back out in the yard, Larry was still arguing with his sister. I don't know what about. But they stopped when they saw me.

"Who was that?" he asked.

"I have an interview on Monday."

"They rang at the door for that?"

"No, they called."

"Wasn't there somebody at the door?"

"Yeah. Some guy selling pencils and wallets."

Larry smiled.

"Oh, I see. An interview in the paper. You haven't even laced up your skates and you're already a star. Watch out it doesn't go to your head."

I didn't let it go to my head. In fact, I wasn't even thinking about it. The tough guy who was looking for Tommy, claiming to be a friend of his cousin's in Baie-Comeau was on my mind. And the guy who was with him…

"What's on your mind?"

"I'm thinking I should find a gym to work out in."

"Isn't there a gym at the Colisée?"

"Yeah … But I want something accessible, close by. I want to be able to go there whenever I feel like it."

"There's a gym not too far away," said Larry's sister.

On my next run, I followed the same route as I had the day before. It went better this time. I wasn't as tired and I cut a minute thirty off the total. For five k's, it wasn't half bad. And come Sunday, at nine o'clock sharp, I walked into the gym on Rue Saint-Joseph. I was the first one there. The gym guy, who had just unlocked the door and turned on the lights, checked me out as he nodded hello, then sat down behind the counter.

He was small, no more than five foot five, dressed in black jogging pants with a white stripe and a black tank-top with the gym logo that showed off his muscular shoulders and bulging biceps. He wasn't tall, but he was very strong and he wanted everyone to know it. You could tell by his face that he was tough. And probably, even though he'd never seen me before, he had issues with guys like me. Because I was just sixteen and I already stood over six feet tall. Whoever I was, I needed to understand that he was the boss, that he was stronger than me, and that I was nothing but a little twerp. So it took him plenty of time to get things organized, to put his chair where he wanted it, shuffle the stack of papers in front of him, check the messages left by the weekend staff, etc. I knew that with an uptight person like him you had to stay calm and never show any impatience. Because if I did, this imbecile would make me wait even longer.

"You have a membership here?" he finally asked me, looking up as though he had just noticed me.

"No."

"Well luckily we're running a special. Thirty dollars for a one-month trial. And after that, if you want to continue, it's $130 for a quarter. A quarter means three months."

He seemed proud to inform me that a quarter was the same as three months. Then he asked if I was familiar with the machines and if I needed a demonstration. I told him that it was all right, I'd figure it out on my own.

The locker room was a bit cramped and smelled strongly of cheap deodorant. There were two rows of lockers and three showers. When I came out, there were videos—with too much pounding bass for my liking—playing on giant screens on all the walls of the gym, the sound all the way up. Two girls, quite a bit older than me, came in and headed over to the tanning salon, which occupied an adjacent room. I hadn't been on the stationary bike for more than five minutes when I saw the same guy enter that had come knocking the day before: Vincent. He handed a bag to the little muscle-man behind the counter, helped himself to an energy drink from the refrigerator and downed it. Then he sat down on the black leather couch next to the counter and began reading a newspaper.

I kept pedalling, my head turned slightly away to avoid meeting his gaze. It wasn't clear to me what I was doing there; I wasn't sure I wanted him to recognize me. But I had forgotten about the big mirrors along the back wall. When I got off the bike, I realized he'd been watching me for a while. When our eyes met, he went back to reading the paper.

I went over to the weight machines and worked my arms, shoulders and chest. After a pretty intense series of sit-ups, lying on a mat with my legs up on a big purple ball, I headed back to the locker room. It had begun to fill up; there were some out-of-shape guys who probably hadn't worked out for a while, but there were also some others with impressive physiques. They spent a lot of time looking at the mirror, fixing their hair, fussing with their t-shirts and shorts. Then, when they were completely satisfied with their look, they ambled out into the gym to begin their daily workout.

I was too shy to take a shower so I made up my mind to grab one at home. On the way out, I gave a nod to the little sourpuss behind the counter. Before I reached the door, big Vincent called out to me:

"Hey, are you Tommy Courchesne's buddy?"

He was still sitting on the black leather sofa, newspaper in his hands, looking me over from head to toe.

"Yes," I said.

"You look like a hockey player."

"I'm starting junior camp tomorrow."

That seemed to get his attention. Because he got up from his seat, tossing his paper on the chair behind him, I noticed that he had a bum knee. Because as soon as he stood up, he started limping and wincing. I guess carrying a ton of muscles put a lot of weight on his long, stringy legs. He shook my hand warmly. His face was as red as my father's and his friends the day after they'd tied one on.

"It's quite an honour to have a future pro among us. I'm Vincent, and I'm a coach and a manager. Do you like it here so far?"

"Yes ..."

"If you ever need anything, you can contact me directly. I've coached several pros."

When I asked who, he tossed out a couple of names I didn't recognize. Guys who made it in the American Hockey League, he said.

"We're like one big happy family around here. Everyone takes pride when one of our own makes it big."

"Okay, cool."

I was already part of the family. He indicated as much by offering to set me up with the same program Tommy

79

had followed at his cousin's gym in Baie-Comeau. I told him I already had a personal trainer and that I'd only be using the gym occasionally, just to stay loose. He raised his eyebrows and then said that was cool.

"It's not easy, what you guys are trying to accomplish. The bar's set high. If things don't work out the way you hope, come and see me."

I nodded okay and then left to go home.

Tommy came in on the bus that night. Larry went to pick him up at the station with Nathalie, who told him he needed to get his Jeep out of the garage as soon as possible because she wasn't going to be providing taxi service much longer. My coach's sister was pretty hard to take. But I must admit that it made me laugh to see him always respond like a dog that's peed on the carpet. Dogs don't really have a sense of right and wrong, but they can tell when they've messed up, just from their master's facial expression and tone of voice. And Larry always answered "yes" to Nathalie, head down, tail tucked between his legs.

Chapter 4

I was glad to see Tommy. I'd only been there three days and already I was sick of Larry and his sister. There was only one thing I wanted: for the hockey season to start, to hit the road and get out of that place as quick as I could. But he barely said hello as he came in, looking disdainfully over his new digs. He tossed his hockey bag down and threw his suitcase onto the bed. He turned to face me, hands on hips. His acne had spread and the pimples on his face were more swollen than before. His muscular arms threatened to burst through the sleeves of his light blue t-shirt. I asked him if he was all right, but he didn't answer. He asked me if a guy named Vincent had been by to see him the night before.

"Yes."

"Did he leave anything for me?" he asked.

"No."

He seemed relieved. Not missing a beat he stuffed his gym clothes into a small backpack and left, saying he was off to the gym. It was nine in the evening. Larry reminded him that camp would start early next morning with tests designed to evaluate the new players' condition and that it might be better for him to conserve his energy. He replied that he was going to keep doing what he had been doing, which so far had gotten results. And

I swear, right then, he shot me a glance. As if to make a point.

I'd make him pay for that, for sure.

That first morning we met the coach, the manager and the coaching staff. Pictures of players and teams who had worn the club's colours in earlier years hung on the locker room walls. We took turns introducing ourselves, like back in grade school. There was a lot of goofing around, some of it pretty funny. There were some serious comedians, real goofs. It lightened up the atmosphere, which was pretty heavy seeing as how we were all rookies. As usual, I didn't have a lot to say when my turn came.

"Hello, I'm Alex. I'm a hockey player."

When the assistant coach asked me if I had anything else to say, I shrugged my shoulders and said no. Everybody cracked up.

Actually, all the guys seemed friendly and easy-going; happy, in any event, just to be there. Everybody except Tommy that is. When his turn came, he blurted out some incomprehensible gibberish. The guys just stared at him. It was the first time I'd ever seen him like that; a guy who in all the time I'd known him had carried himself with supreme confidence, always on top of the situation and never letting anything get to him. Now, he was as red as a tomato and his glistening face made his unsightly acne stand out even more. He scratched his head vigorously, as if he was going to tear his hair out, as he introduced himself, so nervous it was like he was about to faint. The room was silent when he finished; no one could think of anything to say. The discomfort lasted until the assistant coach told us to head over to the weight room for the evaluations.

I did pretty well on the exercises. I was worried how I'd stack up against the other guys, but I could tell that Larry's unorthodox training program had paid off. Because I finished well above average. But it was Tommy who came out on top, far and away. Growling like a demented animal, he worked the treadmill, the stationary bike and the weights longer, faster and with heavier loads than anybody else in camp. In fact, someone told Larry that none of the nineteen- and twenty-year-olds had racked up such impressive results. Really. And while the whole gang was admiring what seemed to them to be an exceptional athlete, when I looked at my buddy, I thought I was looking at the Incredible Hulk.

We were invited to a lunch prepared by volunteers at a banquet hall. The room was decorated with bunting and photos of players who had played for the old Nordiques, most of whom I barely knew since I was just two when the team moved to Colorado. Casually, I checked out the old photos, until my eye fell on one of the largest, my father's favourite player. His hero was a guy from Péribonka, number sixteen, Michel Goulet. Louis, who was a Quebec City fan, told me with a gleam in his eye about the time when a Quebec-Montreal game would get the entire town all worked up. Now, by him, it just wasn't the same anymore. Hockey players were money-making machines that managed their careers like businesses. "There's no heart left in the game."

Everyone was eating sandwiches, drinking sodas and talking. I didn't talk much; mostly I listened. All the noise around me was giving me a headache. Like my father, crowds and tight spaces got on my nerves. But I was also kind of anxious about my upcoming interview with the newspaper. It seemed huge. Papers in Montreal and Quebec had already printed some short articles about me. But this would be the first time I'd be meeting face to face with a journalist, and not some guy from the *Nord-Côtier* or the other weeklies down home. This would be a real interview. I'd have to carry my weight. Except I felt like I didn't really have anything to say. And I didn't think that the newspaper guy was going to find my "hmms," and shrugs terribly interesting for his article. I barely heard what people around me were saying, looking around me, trying to avoid focusing on anybody in particular. Now it was Tommy who was putting on a show; the same guy who was dying of anxiety a couple of minutes before was now speaking with a strong, self-assured voice. Proud of his achievements, he moved onto centre stage. Maybe a bit too much. Because the rudeness that had come over him in the past several months quickly came to the surface. In a loud voice he asked the guys who were listening to him if they'd like to find a place to knock back a couple of cool ones.

Again that feeling of discomfort settled over the room. I guess it was a specialty of his.

For sure the assistant coach and the rest of the coaching staff heard what he said. The guys all quickly shook their heads no; don't count on me, I told him. These were sixteen- and seventeen-year-olds, the camp was their chance of a lifetime. You'd have to be a total jerk to think that after day one of training camp they'd want to go out boozing and partying. And it was on that sour note that our first day of rookie camp came to an end.

I left the banquet hall with him, sure that we'd be pegged as the two hicks from the Côte-Nord. When he asked if I was heading back to the apartment, I told him I was expecting a journalist. No sooner said than the journalist showed up, introduced himself and extended his hand. By the time I turned back around, Tommy had walked off without so much as a nod.

The interview went well. In fact, I had worried for nothing. The reporter, who could have been trying a little too hard to seem friendly, was actually very accommodating. His questions were simple and to the point, and he jotted down all my answers in his notebook. It was no big deal. We talked about one thing or another: my life on the Côte-Nord, my family and my Aboriginal roots. He took a couple of photos with the Colisée rink in the background, and that was it. The next morning, I found out that I was a star player carrying high expectations on my shoulders. In addition to hockey, I loved trout fishing and off-trail riding on my 4 x 4. Wow! What amazing news! I wondered who could be interested in such nonsense. Especially my face in big close-up that covered three quarters of the page.

I spent the rest of the day wandering around, hung out at the mall, then grabbed some poutine at a snack-bar. I didn't really feel like spending the evening with Tommy and Larry. It was dark when I got back to the apartment. As I came up the sidewalk to the house, I could hear a woman yelling. I immediately recognized Nathalie's voice. I paused before opening the door; the living room window was open.

"If you ever pull a stunt like that again, you're out of here! Do you hear me, Laurent?"

Laurent didn't reply. But I could see him in my mind's eye, with his head bowed whenever his older sister chewed him out. After I heard the kitchen door slam and felt sure that scary Nathalie wasn't waiting in the wings, I decided to go in. One thing for sure, I didn't feel at home in the tiny apartment.

Larry was slumped on the couch. He was holding a beer and seemed upset. I didn't have to ask him what had happened. He volunteered.

"Did you hear that?"

"No."

"Liar. I could see your head through the window."

He sighed before taking a sip of beer. But it didn't seem to do anything for him because he put the bottle on the floor and frowned. His red hair was sticking out in all directions. He'd traded his blue jogging suit for jeans and a t-shirt. Usually, when he wasn't wearing sweats it meant he'd been out on a big date.

"I saw my little girl today," he told me with a catch in his voice, like a child who had misbehaved.

"Your daughter? Isn't she in Montreal?"

"Not any more. She lives near here, just a few streets over. I was hanging out close to the school hoping to see her, but her mother, my ex, spotted me. Since she and Nat are good friends, she called to tell her."

Really, I didn't know what to say to Larry. I knew he wasn't allowed to see his daughter. Things like that really make me uncomfortable. All I could do was sit beside him on the couch, and offer him some support just by being there. I think he appreciated it, because he said so, giving me a tap on my thigh as he would have done to a good friend.

"She's going to call the cops on me if I do it again. But I'm not sure I can stop myself."

"You don't have any choice, right?"

"Maybe I'd be better off going back to the Côte-Nord."

I agreed. That's why he'd come to the village in the first place. It's true a coaching position had opened up, but it was mostly because a court order had prevented him from seeing his daughter, for reasons that nobody could understand. I wasn't really in a position to press him for the details, but I could see that the situation— living with an overbearing sister who was also his ex's friend, with his daughter not far away—was more than he could put up with. And I could understand the hang-dog look. The shame. This wasn't the same Larry I knew.

When I asked him where Tommy was, he looked at me as if to say, "where do you think?"

"At the gym?"

"Yeah. I went by the famous gym this morning. It's not too clean, that place. I tried to tell him what I thought of it, but he just laughed in my face."

"He broke all the records today."

"He made sure I knew it, too. I don't want you hanging around there. It's bikers that run that dump. It's nasty. I'd better phone his parents."

I went into my room to pack up my gear. I passed back through the living room as quickly as I could. Larry was up on his feet.

"Where are you going?"

"I'm going to work out at the gym."

I was afraid he was about to freak out. As I closed the door behind me, I could hear him cursing from the other side. I took off on the run; no way I wanted to deal with him. I absolutely had to speak with my buddy. ·

On edge, I opened the door to the gym. A blast of moist air and music cranked up to the max hit me in the face. A video of some stupid pop group was playing on all the monitors. Monday was a busy day, it seemed; the place was humming. All the machines were in use. Sweat was oozing out of every pore and the big windows facing the street were all fogged up; all you could see were the headlights of the cars going by on Rue Saint-Joseph.

It was my second visit. When he saw me, the cranky little guy at the reception desk was surprisingly friendly. He even got up to shake my hand. Don't worry about how crowded it was, he said. It was past nine o'clock, the place would soon empty out and I'd have the weight room to myself. Did I want an energy drink? It was on the house. I took a pass, thanked him, and walked slowly to the locker room, looking around the weight room as I passed through, but Tommy was nowhere to be seen. He wasn't in the locker room, either. The guy at the reception desk was right. The gym emptied and everyone converged on the lockers. The small room was soon packed with muscular guys, fat guys, skinny guys.

It was impossible to move. The place stank of cheap perfume and sweat. I wedged into a corner near three rusty old lockers, next to a steel door beneath a red Exit sign. I stood in my corner with my back to the crowd, facing the dirty yellow wall. Overhead hung neon lights, their electrical connections drooping from the missing tiles in the drop ceiling. What was I doing there, I wondered. I was suffocating, dizzy. The air was stale. There wasn't any space. I closed my eyes and imagined tall black spruces at the summit of a large hill that I had to climb by grabbing hold of the roots protruding from the ground. A big oaf who was admiring his muscles pushed me aside as if I weren't even there. I hadn't noticed I was standing in front of a mirror; I felt totally ridiculous. Unable to tolerate my surroundings for another moment, I pushed on the exit-bar of the steel door, quickly closed it behind me and left.

I found myself in a dark hallway lit by a single red bulb. There was a large hamper full of towels. Off to the side were some black garbage bags, cardboard boxes, and tools scattered on a table. On my left, a door opened to the outside. As I headed for it I heard voices on my right, and noticed a staircase leading to the basement.

That was when I realized I'd left my backpack in the locker room. But the sound of voices from below diverted my attention. I edged down the stairs on tiptoe, my hand sliding along the steel handrail. At the very bottom, a narrow shaft of light shone through an open door. When I recognized Vincent's unpleasant voice, I froze, unable to take another step, terrified of being caught by the sniffling brute who spoke like a retard.

My heart began to hammer in my chest when, in answer to a question from Vincent, I heard the voice of my friend Tommy reply.

Right then, I couldn't figure out the nature of their conversation nor what they were talking about exactly. But this is pretty much what I heard:

"It's your liver. Your cousin gave you some pills to take. They're hard on the system. With intramuscular injections, you'll give your liver a break and your symptoms will disappear, you'll see."

"Okay," answered Tommy. "Uh … Where are you going to stick that thing?"

"In your ass!" replied a gruff voice I didn't recognize.

The same person broke into a booming laugh, which quickly transformed into a wracking cough that took a while to subside. Finally, the man cleared his throat and hawked. Vincent went on with what he was saying.

"The injection has to go into a large muscle so that your body can absorb the dose slowly. We could stick you in the shoulder or thigh if you want. But a shot in the butt is more discreet, when it comes to the marks."

I'd heard everything they said, but I had to see it with my own eyes. I knew I would be taking a terrible risk by sticking my head into the room. But I couldn't believe my ears. I had to get to the bottom of it. It all seemed so scary, so twisted. I just couldn't believe that Tommy was mixed up in something like that.

I slid my arm through the crack of the door … halfway to my elbow. I figured if anyone saw my hand, I could scramble back up the stairs and escape through the exit. I slowly wiggled my arm and seeing as how

Vincent continued talking as though he hadn't noticed, I held my breath and peeked through the door.

The basement had a cement floor and there were things piled everywhere: furniture, rugs, old weight machines and exercise gear. There were different-shaped lockers, and on the ground, parts that seemed to have come from some gas-powered bicycles; a little bit as though someone had taken apart two or three Harleys and spread the parts out on the floor. In the centre of all the mess, under the murky glare of a flickering neon light, stood Vincent. Sitting in front of him on a chair was the bearded guy wearing a red, white and blue scarf. And, standing between the two nasties, one knee resting on an exercise bench, was Tommy.

He seemed hesitant, a bit lost. He loosened his belt and let his jeans fall loosely below his waist. Vincent took a small brown vial from a table next to him, stuck in the syringe and extracted the fluid. The black-bearded guy with the all-American scarf finished rolling a cigarette, sucking it into his mouth two or three times to moisten it. As Tommy leaned forward, exposing his right buttock to big Vincent who was eyeing the tip of the needle, the bearded man lit the cigarette, which turned out to be a very large joint. He exhaled the smoke, which began to curl upward under the neon light.

"You want a puff?" asked the man, handing the joint to Tommy, who didn't know what to say, being on all fours and in a humiliating position.

"Hey, you brain-dead loser!" said Vincent to his friend. "The guy's an athlete. He's just started junior training camp and you want him to smoke some weed?"

The other guy shrugged his shoulders and took another puff, while Vincent jabbed the needle into Tommy's backside. I saw my friend grip the exercise bench, grimacing slightly. Then, suddenly, he turned in my direction.

Our eyes met and immediately locked on one another. The horrible truth hit us, as if we both understood how serious, how grave it was; something had broken forever. I pulled my head back behind the door as Tommy let out a cry of astonishment, or maybe, of rage.

Petrified, I couldn't move. And in the distance, I'm sure I heard wolves howling.

"What's the matter?" said Vincent.

"Uh ... nothing, it hurts, that's all."

"You're crying over a shot in the bum? How are you going to handle playing in the juniors?"

And then, as the gruesome laughter of the guy with the beard burst out anew, I flew up the stairs four at a time and pushed open the steel door at the end of the hallway.

I emerged into a dark, quiet side street. The street-lights cast long shadows from the rubbish bins onto the grey asphalt. Without a moment's hesitation, I took off running at full speed, up the street and then turning down the adjacent boulevard. Wolves were howling from every corner of the city, the sound rising up from the end of every alley, from every street around me. My heart was pounding deep in my chest. I ran with my head thrust back, my antlers thrust back, my warm breath steaming through my nostrils, my steps driven by the heart of a desperate animal running wild through the city. The moose I had become sprinted between the people on the sidewalk, as if dashing between the black spruce of a dense forest. And the wolves were getting closer and closer. Only at the last minute did I realize that I was about to crash into a red brick wall at the end of the street. I leaped, and extended one leg. Then I turned around, back against the wall. Looking for a way out, I spotted two police cars tearing down a side street to my right, sirens wailing.

The street stretched out before me; far off I saw a church steeple and lights twinkling in store windows. Every time I banged my head against the wall, memories of Tommy and me on the Côte-Nord tumbled down from the stars like a meteor shower. Riding on our ski-doos in winter, lost on trails we had never been on before. Me on my quad trying to keep up with him as he drove his dirt bike at full speed along the dunes over-looking the sea. And above all, that unforgettable moment last winter in the school cafeteria when he came over and sat down beside me after I'd run my skidoo into the river at twenty below. He didn't say a word. We just laughed, cracking jokes. Guys don't talk about these things, ever. Yet everything was okay; there was nothing to worry about.

Larry was in bed by the time I got home. I couldn't be bothered to take a shower and plopped into bed. It was hot in my little room, but I closed the window any-way. It was like I didn't want to hear anything, or maybe like I was afraid of something. When I closed the blinds, I saw eyes gleaming orange in the dark among the tomato plants and the beanstalks in Nathalie's garden. Watching me. Waiting for me.

Tommy came in an hour later. I was still awake. Scrunched down under the covers, listening, I tracked his heavy footsteps in the kitchen, which was right next to my bedroom. He went to the bathroom to pee. Then to the fridge for a glass of milk. Through the opening at the bottom of my bedroom door, I saw the light go out. Everything fell still. Then, slowly, he came up to my door; then stopped in front of it.

What was he doing? Did he want to talk? I thought he was about to knock, but he didn't, completely silent and motionless. I could almost hear him breathing on the other side. After a wait that seemed interminable, I began to sit up in bed, slowly, careful not to make a sound. A long bead of sweat trickled down my chest. I don't know how much time passed while he stood outside my door, but it was crazy long. Sitting on the edge of my bed, my feet on the linoleum floor, I was ready to defend myself. But I was afraid. Afraid that he had talked with Vincent and his joint-smoking sidekick. And that they told him to settle accounts with me. Or that they were even actually out there, in the back yard, lurking in the shadows, hiding among the tomatoes, waiting for just the right moment to pounce on me.

Finally he moved. I was all set to jump to my feet to take away the advantage of surprise. But to my relief, he went back to his room. He closed the door gently, and then I heard him fooling around for a while before hitting the sack. I jammed a chair under the doorknob to bar the door. Was it possible that he just wanted to clear the air? Should I take the initiative and go to him? But what was there to say? There was no denying what had passed between us when our eyes met. The surprise and shame in his. The surprise and distress in mine.

I knew I'd never be able to fall asleep. After tossing and turning over a dozen times in the space of five minutes, I rose and grabbed my laptop. The screen was blinding and splashed its bright white light all over my body. My abs were sharply defined under the glowing light. I had changed. It was two o'clock in the morning. I wrote a short message to Chloé, saying I missed her and was thinking of her. It was only then that I fell asleep.

In the morning I awoke with a start, drenched in sweat. My window was closed and the heat was already overwhelming. Larry knocked on my door saying it was time. I dressed in a hurry and looked for my backpack. My heart sank when I realized I had left it at the gym the day before.

Not a word was spoken around the breakfast table. Tommy and I were avoiding eye contact. I expected Larry to say something about the hangdog look on our faces. But he seemed caught up in his own concerns, and said nothing.

"You're not having anything to eat?" I finally asked, breaking the uneasy silence that prevailed in the small apartment.

"No," he replied, leaning on the counter, a cup of coffee in one hand. "I'm not really hungry."

It was hot. Through the window screen, I could hear Nathalie out in the garden yelling at her kids, who were already quarreling at half past seven in the morning. I imagined the neighbours who had to put up with those

95

little loudmouths 365 days a year, shaking their heads and sighing in resignation. The linoleum in the apartment was disgusting: whole pieces had been torn out, showing the greasy particle board underneath. The refrigerator was leaking, forming a puddle on the floor that a grungy mop was waiting to swab up.

I could only think of one thing: find another place to live. There was no way it was going to work out for me here. I needed to concentrate on my game. That was all that mattered. I had to put Tommy and his cheating ways out of my mind. It turned my stomach to think that he was making himself sick, really sick, just to boost his performance. I needed to try to talk to him, I couldn't just ignore it. Later on, we found ourselves alone in the locker room at the Colisée. The other guys were already on the ice. Without mentioning or planning anything, as if we both knew it was the right time, each of us lagged behind. Me by suddenly discovering that I needed to change my laces while Tommy had to retape the blade of his hockey stick.

There were just the two of us, plus a janitor who was cleaning the showers on the other side. Tommy still hadn't looked at me. I could see he wasn't going to make the first move. So I did. I went over to him. Concentrating on his hockey stick, looking for the best angle to apply the tape, he avoided looking at me. But he was listening. I felt nervous. Sweat was pouring off him. As usual, his face, covered with aggressive and purulent acne, was as red as ever. He was big, strong and more powerful than ever. But never had he seemed so fragile.

"Listen, Tom …"

"What?" he interjected, without giving me the chance to finish my sentence.

"… it's just that, I'm worried about you."

"Yeah, well I'm worried about you. You better watch out where you're sticking your big nose."

It was a threat. I couldn't believe my ears. It was me that did something wrong. It was me that stuck my nose into his business.

"What are you doing? You were always a good hockey player. You don't need…."

"Need what?"

"Umm …"

"What? What are you talking about?"

I couldn't say it. I just couldn't find the words. All of a sudden, it all seemed unreal; as if nothing ever happened. As if the sordid scene in the basement of the gym had never happened. And since I wasn't talking, it was Tommy's turn. He tossed the roll of tape into his locker and pointed his stick at me. All he could get past his lips was a groan. His light-coloured eyes were damp with tears that never fell. And he growled like a bear as he left, slamming the locker room door behind him.

On the ice, the coach and the coaching staff explained what we were going to be doing that week. The cuts would be coming soon. Pay close attention to instructions, they told us; they wouldn't be cutting us any slack. The bottom line was that there were really only three forward and one defenceman's slots open. I figured I had a good shot at it.

I dominated in the power skating exercises, handling them better than anyone. Except near the end when

Tommy, never short of breath, began to get the upper hand. A guy from Abitibi, one of the clowns at the team lunch the day before, was pretty hard to beat in the skills tests. But again, I came out all right. Leaning against the boards while I caught my breath, I watched Tommy going through his paces, looking clumsy. It was definitely not his strong point. During the one-on-ones he had to shove a couple of guys in order to get where he was going, which earned him a couple of comments from the coaches. He lost his temper and whacked the boards two or three times with his stick.

I handled the one-timers with flying colours. I had a wicked shot, and was able to put the puck on the target wherever they asked me, no problem. There were guys up in the stands taking notes and I knew I was getting high marks. In fact, everything was going easier than I had expected.

Things went a little downhill for me when we started team exercises. I found myself playing against Tommy— a fate that was to dog me all the way to the end of training camp. Not only that, it turned out that he lined up right opposite me. At the faceoff, I felt his shoulder leaning heavily against mine. He was letting me know he wasn't going to be holding back. I tried to push back, but he refused to budge. Okay, game on. Twice I went up the wing and turned up the jets just in time to avoid his check, and heard him hit the boards with a crash. On my third rush, I had to keep my eyes on the puck; it was bouncing and I had trouble controlling it. That's when he got me. But good. Boom! I thought my head would pop. I could swear everybody in the stands watching the workout rose from their seats at the moment of impact. Stunned, I put one knee on the ice to get my bearings. I managed to pull myself together and finish the game with a couple of half-decent plays. But it was like I was running on empty. Plus I had a splitting headache.

In the locker room, I was seated on the bench. I could hardly move a muscle.

"McKenzie, keep your head up," said one of the guys.

"You gave us a scare," said Tommy, who was awkwardly trying to show some sympathy.

He was trying to show that it was just part of the game, that he was a decent guy. And even if he could get some people to swallow it, I wasn't biting. I cut him a sideways glance and asked him how his right buttock was feeling. Nobody understood a word I was talking about. But Tom, his eyes darkening, knew exactly what I meant.

A trainer came to look me over. He sat next to me and asked if I was going to be okay. I told him I had a bit of a headache, but that was all. He said it would be better to go to the hospital and see a doctor. His name was François. He was a nurse studying physical fitness at Laval University. On the way to the hospital, he asked me if I'd known Tommy for long. I told him that we knew each other since we were six. We went to grade school and high school together, and we were always on the same hockey teams. Right into juniors.

"Quite an athlete, your friend."

"Yeah …"

"A tough guy."

I had never been so ready to tell someone the truth about what was going on. François looked like someone who might be able to help Tom out. I wanted to tell him that Tommy had always been cool, an easy-going kind of guy, the kind of guy who always came out on top, thanks to his love of the game and his desire to win. Now, what used to be pleasure or desire had morphed into a pure and senseless rage. He hadn't been like this before. But, once again, I held my silence. I stood mutely beside the trainer, looking at my feet and the Saint-François Hospital waiting room floor.

The doctor examined my eyes and ears. He asked me some questions and sent me home. I didn't have a concussion. I didn't have any symptoms. But if, later in the day, I experienced dizziness, nausea or confusion, I was to come back and see him.

Larry was sitting on a lawn chair at the back of the yard reading the paper. After dropping my stuff off in my room, I glanced into Tommy's. It was completely empty. His suitcase, his things, everything was gone. He'd even made the bed.

I pulled up a chair and sat down next to Larry. I took off my running shoes and socks and wriggled my feet in the fresh-cut grass. Laptop perched on my knees, I had to fight the glare in order to read the screen. There were a couple of emails in my Hotmail account, including one from Chloé. She was thinking of me too, she wrote. She added that she would try to make it to Quebec City in a couple of weeks, but she didn't know exactly when. She might be able to take a couple of days off after school started. She signed off with a couple of xx's, after asking me to say hi to Tommy for her.

"Where'd he go?" I asked.

"He left," answered Larry.

"What do you mean, he left? Left for where?"

"I called his mom to say I was worried about him. But all she did was throw insults at me, like how I was a complete idiot who was ruining her kid's chances of success. I don't have a clue what Tommy told her. She just yelled at me and refused to listen to a thing I had to say. He packed up after I hung up and went to stay with a friend of his cousin's."

I had no doubt that the friend was Vincent.

When Larry got up to go inside, a piece of paper slid from the chair and landed in the grass at my feet. I picked it up. It was a pretty good crayon sketch of Larry's face. It wasn't hard to recognize his red hair, his peaked forehead, his glasses perched precariously on his stub nose. At the bottom, to the right, "I love you, papa" was written.

Later that evening, I had to return an urgent call from my father. Tommy's mother was stirring up the village, claiming that Larry had gone crazy and was taking it out on us. I tried to calm things down, pointing out that it wasn't really working out for Tommy at training camp and that he had it in for everybody. He was convinced that his problems were due to Larry's negative influence. When my father heard what I had to say, he seemed reassured. He made a few suggestions which I immediately forgot, and passed the phone to Sylvie. It made me a little sad to hear my aunt's voice. Right at that moment,

I would have given anything to be with her. Because with her, nothing was really complicated; she took it all with a grain of salt. Were things going good? For sure. Was everything okay? Yeah, yeah, okay. Are you happy? For sure, Sylvie, I'm really happy. I'm having a good camp. I'm confident I'll make the team. Maybe that's why Tommy was so angry at Larry. Maybe it's because things weren't going the way he wanted.

"Can't you help him? Talk to him?"

"I've tried. But he's pretty thick-headed. I can't skate and score for him."

"Just the same, Alex…"

I could stay with a girlfriend of hers in Charlesbourg, a suburb north of Quebec City. There was a room in the basement. I'd have all the privacy I needed. And it would certainly be quieter than being downtown, wouldn't it?

That was exactly what I'd been wishing for the day before. But everything had changed. Tommy had split, and I really thought that Larry needed my help, and more than that, my presence. While my friend had gone over the line, having steroids injected in his bum by a handful of bikers, my coach was standing right on that line, spying on his own daughter at her school. I imagined Larry decked out in a grey raincoat, a fake beard and oversized sunglasses, being pulled over in his Jeep by the police. That's the reason I turned down Sylvie's offer. But I did promise her I'd think about it, and that maybe, once the season was over, I'd take her up on it. But not before. I didn't have time for that right now. I had to concentrate on hockey.

After I hung up I noticed that Larry had made himself scarce. Maybe he was afraid he'd have to talk to my father and that'd he'd get another earful.

I spent the rest of the evening slouched on the sofa, watching television and surfing the Internet. I tried to find Chloé on Skype or MSN, but she wasn't on-line on either one.

No, Larry hadn't gone crazy. He was sure that something was out of synch with Tom. Especially after he paid a visit to the gym and got a look at the seedy guys who ran the place. He just tried to do the right thing. What's more, finding out that people in the village were talking behind his back, and that Tommy's mother was bad-mouthing him was unbearable. There already wasn't much left of his reputation after his various run-ins with the law and his employers; if people were going to think he was a lousy coach and an unworthy mentor, there wouldn't be anything left for him to do except go back into the army and disappear forever into the mountains of Afghanistan.

That's why, that very evening, he headed over to the gym to have it out with Tommy. He wanted to confront him in front of the guys who were leading him down the road to ruin. And who, in doing so, were destroying him forever by turning him into a monster.

Monday was a busy night. Tuesday was even more so. The music was thumping, the atmosphere stifling, and people were lined up in front of the machines. Larry quickly spotted Tommy at the back of the room, in the corner where the weights and dumbbells were stacked. Vincent was beside him, egging him on as he power lifted.

Our coach wasn't a big guy. But he wasn't afraid of anybody. He'd been to war, and no doped-up body builder was going to intimidate him. Without a glance at the jittery little guy at the reception desk, Larry marched with a determined stride to the back of the room.

Vincent immediately spotted the bizarre individual heading straight for him. Of course, Larry was decked out in his pale blue jogging suit. With his blue shades and his unkempt red hair sticking out in all directions, he was hard to miss. A man of action who was used to all sorts of nasty business, Vincent hurriedly helped Tommy lower the steel bar and its enormous cast iron plates. He knew exactly who he was dealing with.

"Tom," said Larry, "I know what's going on here. I want to talk to you."

Tommy was about to reply, but Vincent abruptly cut him off.

"Hey, my friend, none of this concerns you. Butt out. Just a bit of friendly advice."

"I'm not talking to you, fat ass. Which means … just shut your mouth!" During his stint in the Canadian armed forces, Larry had taken some judo courses. When Vincent, spitting nails, moved in to grab him, Larry flipped him over his hip with a lightning-fast move. The body builder with the bulging biceps went crashing to the mat. Cool as a cucumber, our coach turned to Tommy and pointed his finger at him, commanding him to get out of this dump. Immediately!

No talking back. And I think Tom just might have obeyed him, and that Larry might have been able to get through to him. It was just possible that all he needed was an authority figure who stood taller than him, and could upend with a single judo throw the man in whom Tom had placed all his trust. But with Vincent still writhing on the floor in pain after crushing his weak and undersized hips beneath the weight of his top heavy mass, Larry had imprudently turned his back on the guy at the front desk. The thug, himself a martial arts enthusiast, had grabbed a pair of nunchucks from under the counter. He exploded into the air and delivered a violent kick between Larry's shoulders, sending him to the floor. After a dozen nunchuck blows, Larry found himself being dragged across the gym carpet and tossed outside by a couple of brutes who outdid each other finishing him off. They left him there, unconscious, between two dumpsters on Rue Notre-Dame-des-Anges.

"But I didn't really lose consciousness," he said, sitting on a chair in front of me, his face battered, one eye swollen under his blue shades, a bag of ice on his head. "I was faking."

He was faking… What a strategy. But one that had served him well. Because the toughs, afraid they had gone too far and worried about having a death on their consciences, had finally left him alone.

I'd been asleep on the couch when he stumbled in somewhere around 11 p.m. As soon as I saw him, I leapt to my feet to give him a place to sit down. But he asked for a chair because his kidneys were hurting. He gingerly sat down, while I went to get some ice. A lot of good it did me to ask him questions; he could only moan in response. He sat there a long moment unable to speak, legs stretched out on the coffee table. Then he opened his eyes, as if it was all coming back to him.

"I tried talking to Tommy, but it didn't do any good."

That much was clear. Then he gave me a blow-by-blow account. He seemed proud of pretending to be close to death, throwing the guys who had beaten him into a bit of a panic. As if he had gotten the best of them.

"Should we call the cops?"

"The police?" he said. "What's the use?"

He didn't like the police. In fact, he was afraid of them. What he hadn't mentioned was that they'd paid him a visit, a couple of days before. His ex had called the police after seeing him watching his daughter, Melissa, in the schoolyard. Which was why his sister had blown her stack.

Larry got up with a long sigh, his face twisted with pain, and shuffled off to his room. But before he did, he reached for the handset on the small end-table beside the couch. He held it to his ear, and then handed it to me.

"There's a message. You listen to it. I don't have the heart to hear it. It's probably Tommy's mother threatening to sue me for harassing her kid."

As he disappeared into his room, I played back the recording and listened to the message. It had probably come in during the afternoon. I recognized Vincent's disagreeable voice right away.

"Hey, champ. Someone found your backpack in the locker room yesterday evening. You can come by anytime. It's in my office."

The next day, I woke up in a bad mood. Another night spent tossing and turning, wondering how I was going to retrieve my backpack. After what I'd witnessed in the gym basement—that is, if Tommy had even mentioned seeing me—and with the beating Larry had taken, I figured I was less than welcome. If I showed up, I might even end up in a dumpster myself.

Despite his wretched appearance and his aching body, Larry insisted on driving me to the Colisée. I could have grabbed a taxi, but he said he felt it was his responsibility. We drove in silence in his Jeep, stuck in traffic, blocked by some road pavers. Every time he stepped on the clutch to change gears, he leaned slightly to his left and clenched his teeth. When he left me off at the door, he asked if I minded if he skipped the workout. He wanted to go to the clinic to see a doctor. He thought he might have a broken rib. Not to worry I told him, everything was going to be okay.

"You should call Nathalie. She'll pick you up."

I declined, insisting that I'd figure something out.

Even though my legs were wooden and my breath was shorter than usual, I did pretty well. My passes were sharp, right on the stick, my shots on the net, and even if I was a step slower than usual, I was pretty fluid on my skates.

And that was how things stayed all week, until Thursday, the second-to-last day of rookie camp.

Over those three days, I battled Tommy as hard as I could. I kept my eye on him and gave him as little space as possible. And I seized every opportunity to make him look bad. When they put him out on my line, I'd zip him a wicked pass right on the money, but with enough on it that I knew he wouldn't be able to handle it; stick-handling just wasn't his strength. When he was lined up against me, I took a great deal of pleasure blowing past him on the left, knowing that he couldn't pivot on that leg. Easy moves for me that really got under his skin. We exchanged a few hits, and even though he was too strong for me, a sense of rage would well up in me whenever I spotted him anywhere near me. I was developing quite a burn.

"Hey, Jolly Green Giant. Take the right pills this morning?"

He lost his head trying to tear mine off and I came out of the corner with the puck looking for the pass. It clicked every time. At wit's end, he took it out on anybody he could find, serving up a dangerous cross-check that just about got him tossed. The coach took him aside for a talking to. Tommy, sweat dripping down, listened attentively, nervously nodding his head. He shifted his weight from one foot to the other like an animal set to pounce. After the tête-à-tête we all thought he'd step it down a notch. But no. He fought twice, inflicting some serious damage on a couple of guys who came after him after he taunted them.

It was clear that if he wasn't going to win a spot on the strength of his play, he'd win it on strength alone, even if it meant becoming a goon. Besides, everyone—coaches and players—now clearly saw him in that role. Some of the guys were scared enough to keep a healthy distance, even after practice, as if he was a grizzly in a cage.

Partly, that made me feel better. Too bad for him. I continued to play my game. I was there to score goals and I was the best. I put five in the net including two on breakaways to lead my team to a 7-2 victory. There weren't many people in the stands, but quite a few were yelling my name every time I touched the puck. And real training camp hadn't even started yet. No doubt I'd be making the place explode this winter. A couple of good-looking blondes caught my eye.

The coaches didn't have much to say. Which seemed like a good sign. If they came up to me, it was to congratulate me or to give me some very specific technical advice: on how to position myself when we were practicing one of their game systems.

"Do you understand what I'm trying to say?" asked Carl, the assistant. "If you quit your position too soon, all it takes is a quick turnover and you're out of the game. Look for the pass, but stay closer to the blue line. Stay on your man, got it?"

He was speaking to me, but all I could hear were the girls yelling my name.

Tommy and a few others were being watched more closely. And obviously, that was also a good thing. If they had the coach's eye, it was for good reasons. You could tell most of the rest of the guys knew they weren't going to make it. I felt a slight tug at my heart when stick-handling around them as if they were orange cones. But I knew only too well that I had to be ruthless. For at the first opportunity, they'd be the same way towards me.

Practice was over and I was coming out of the showers when I saw Tommy coming in from the rink. As usual, he'd been putting in overtime. He was all red, out of breath. He sat down on the bench in front of his locker.

Then he doubled over, clutching his stomach. Carl and François were talking in a corner, and some other guys were still getting dressed. I approached him.

"Is everything okay, Tom?"

He looked up at me. It was the first time I noticed how yellow he looked. He took a deep breath, as though trying to stifle his pain, then he shook his head left to right in a clear no.

"Are you sure?"

Once again he nodded his head to say he was all right.

"Maybe you should see François."

And with that, he exploded, slamming the bench with his fist, and telling me to mind my own business.

"Everything okay, guys?" asked François, with Carl at his side.

I nodded that it was. We were just fooling around. Right, Tom? Right, he mumbled.

I got dressed, leaving Tommy alone in his corner, and left, accompanied by the two guys from Abitibi. I was pretty sure one of them, Danny, was going to make the team. He was a tall, skinny defenceman who handled his position quite well. He read my fakes better than anybody else and forced me to pass the puck, preventing me from going to the net. When a forward sees a defenceman and already has it in his head that it'll be hard to beat him, it gives the defence a distinct advantage in the game of momentum that we call hockey.

The other guy, Yannick, was probably going to be cut. He hung a few steps behind us as we walked, silent; probably realizing that his beautiful dream of making it in juniors would be nothing but a dream for yet another year. He was nineteen. For sure, it must have been discouraging to watch a sixteen-year-old like myself totally in command on the ice while he had to struggle just to stay in the game. Competition, in all its forms, is a cold-hearted beast. But it can also be a real motivator. Like what I was facing in Tommy. Someone, somewhere, must have an idea of what he was doing, because never had I felt such a rage, such a desire to outdo myself. And it came from the desire to annihilate the other. Disturbing, but terribly effective.

Yannick made a comment about two girls who were headed our way: short skirts, tank tops and bright loafers. Very sexy. I immediately recognized the two girls in the bleachers who had been hollering my name and, in my usual way—super cool, kind of embarrassed—I was about to move past them, my hands in my pockets, eyes to the ground, when one of them spoke to me with a great deal of familiarity.

I looked up and immediately recognized her. But she had changed so much that I would have needed binoculars to have known it was her up in the stands. A flood of emotions welled up in me, I couldn't say a word.

"What's the big deal? ... It's me, Jess!"

It really was Jessie. Except that with her frizzy hair, short skirt and wearing a ton of makeup, I didn't know how to react. I held out my arms. She leapt into my embrace and squeezed me tight.

"Umm... Hi," I said.

"Umm... Umm... Umm. You're still the same!" she exclaimed, laughing and pushing away from me with both hands.

She was very pretty. And her friend, every bit as much. I had earned my teammates' admiration for my on-ice exploits. But now they were burning with pure envy, and I had to laugh. Danny and Yannick hung back a few steps, waiting for me to make the introductions. They seemed just as intimidated as I was. And when time came for them to leave, I could tell how unhappy they were.

Jessie's friend was named Vicky. She was tall, slender, and seemed really laid-back. She stood with her shoulders relaxed, one hand on her hip, the other holding a pink leather handbag. The sun beat down on us in the Colisée's huge parking lot.

Jess took me by the arm.

"I'm happy to see you," she said.

"Me, too," I replied.

"I couldn't believe it when I saw you in the paper! I told Vicky, 'Hey, I know him! We've got to go see him.'"

The far end of a dirt road on the Côte-Nord and Quebec City's Limoilou district were worlds apart. And Jessie seemed to embrace both those disparate and contrasting worlds. I had known her as someone quiet and reserved. After all the craziness of the previous winter I had given up hope of ever seeing her again. In spite of her drinking, and the bitter taste that remained from our one and only kiss, I still had fond memories of her, even if they were a bit idealized. Now, I found her completely different, as if she had jumped straight out of a YouTube clip. A little too ordinary for my liking. But ever since I had arrived in town I had been bored out of my mind. Larry was pitiful and Tommy even more so. It seemed like Chloé was at the other end of the world.

In fact, I didn't have any friends and I spent most of my time, at least when I wasn't working out, completely alone with nothing to do. The three previous evenings I had spent in the little five and a half on Rue du Roi had been the worst. After watching every hockey and street fighting video I could find on the Internet and then watching any old movie I could find on TV, I was ready to fall for somebody from back home.

She seemed truly happy to see me. She was sincere, in any case. And perhaps, deep down, she was bored herself. She asked after just about everyone she knew, even Chloé.

"She's doing all right," I reassured her.

"Are you guys going out together? I heard it on the grapevine."

"A few times, over the summer. But it didn't really click."

I had Jessie in my arms, but I couldn't help discreetly glancing over at big tall Vicky, walking along on my left. She gave an extra little swing of her hips as she moved, constantly fiddling with her oversized sunglasses in their white plastic frames.

We walked on until we came to an old grey rusted-over Tercel, waiting in a parking lot.

"You want a ride? It's her mother's car."

I said yes, and climbed into the back. It smelled like bubble gum and gas fumes. Vicky started the motor, which coughed and sputtered while Jess turned around in the front seat to continue our conversation. It seemed strange that since we had met at the Colisée exit, Vicky hadn't spoken a word.

"What are you doing this afternoon?" asked Jessie.

"I'm going running."

"Running? Didn't you just finish practice?"

"Yes. But I run after."

"You athletes are nuts. Where do you run?"

"Victoria Park. Then I take the path to Cartier-Brébeuf and circle across the river to Marie-de-l'Incarnation."

"Cartier-Brébeuf… The park in Limoilou? That's near where we live. We were just headed over there to work on our tans."

Chapter 5

Vicky could barely handle her mother's car. At every stop sign and after every red light she popped the clutch and the old heap lurched forward. But now we were rolling, windows down, me slouched down in the back seat, eyes moving from Jess's blond curls to Vicky's long, bleached windblown hair. It was like floating on a cloud.

Jessie kept twisting in her seat to offer me gum or a cigarette, which I naturally refused. The sun full in my face, I stared at the brightly dressed denizens of the Basse-Ville that crowded the sidewalks. Quebec City seemed to me to be the most beautiful town in the world. While the Côte-Nord, so far away, was becoming a distant memory. Riding through the woods in my quad, going fishing, the forests and the lakes, had become abstractions far from the happiness I was experiencing at that moment. Nothing else mattered.

Jessie was looking me steadily in the eye. And I held her gaze, smiling nonchalantly. She was incredibly beautiful. She talked about everything under the sun, gesticulating this way and that. I couldn't understand a word she was saying, on account of the wind and the music. But I didn't care. I was feeling fine.

We whipped around the corner onto Rue du Roi, just about smacking into a cyclist and running over three pedestrians. Vicky seemed oblivious to everything, as though she owned the road, flicking the finger at anyone who dared say something about her driving.

"Here," I said, "right next to the park."

She simply looked at me in the rear-view mirror, without a word, finally bringing the old Tercel to a stop right at my door. This girl seemed incapable of speaking.

I got out of the car and went into my apartment like a man on a mission. In my room, I grabbed a pair of black shorts, a white t-shirt and my running shoes. As I still hadn't been able to get up the courage to retrieve my backpack from big Vince's office, I decided I'd borrow one of Larry's. I rummaged through the mess scattered around his bed: pale blue sweats, dirty socks and some gross white underwear with skid marks… Yuck. All that unpleasant effort and still no pack. In the closet I found a backpack on the top shelf. I grabbed one of the straps and pulled it down. A pile of old towels hidden behind it tumbled to the floor. There was a dull thunk, as if something really heavy was inside the towels. As I picked it up I felt a very hard object through the fabric. Unrolling the towels, I found a gun.

It was black, a revolver. The handle was made of hardwood and was missing a whole section; it wasn't exactly new. The barrel was stubby. On it, you could still read the engraving: Smith and Wesson, .357 Magnum.

I was stunned to find such a weapon hidden in his things, in the room right next to mine. What was he going to do with it? He had a troubled past, some run-ins with authorities that he dragged along behind him like a ball and chain. It was an unthinkable risk for a guy like him to be caught with a piece like that. And I didn't even dare to think about the whole situation with his ex who forbade him to see his daughter. It was impossible for me to imagine he'd want to use it. Impossible.

The kitchen door swung open and then slammed shut with a bang. Someone had come in. I couldn't let Larry see me with the gun in my hand. Hurriedly, I rewrapped the weapon. I was still stretching as high as I could reach, arms fully extended in the closet, when I sensed someone nearby. Standing in the doorway, Nathalie was watching me, her arms folded over her chest. She had on her hiking boots and sported a khaki fisherman's cap on her head.

"What are you doing?"

"I was looking for a backpack," I said, pointing to the old backpack I had found. "I lost mine."

"Laurent isn't with you?"

"Ahh… no."

"Did he go along with you on your workout?"

"Uhh… no. He hasn't been for a couple of days."

I admit it, it wasn't too swift. Now she was really fuming. It would have been so easy to say, "Yes, he was with me. But he had to go to the pharmacy for something, he'll be back soon." But I felt cornered, trapped, caught with the handgun. It was a lie, but I had to protect it. So instinctively, I began to tell every half-truth that popped into my head, hoping to keep the existence of the revolver secret.

Nathalie began to rant, consumed with rage, huge tears running down her cheeks.

"He'd better not be pulling his old shit anymore! I know exactly why he came to stay here. But I'm telling you, that's not going to happen! Not in my house. I never want to see that damned maniac again. Never!"

Outside, the two girls, tired of waiting, honked the horn a couple of times. Nathalie was still crying. The horn of the Tercel honked again. And I decided to take care of job one. The two girls. I brushed past Nathalie and left the room, exiting by the back door.

As I shut the door behind me and was crossing the street, I heard her yelling through the window:

"That goes for the two of you too! Get the hell out of here!"

I jumped into the car, and Vicky gave it the gas.

Just as they were about to drop me off at Victoria Park, I told them that I'd like to go to Cartier-Brébeuf Park with them. I'd do four or five laps of the park and that would be enough of a workout. Jessie was pleased. Vicky, still wordless, turned the car around. I couldn't tell if the pouting expression on her face, which I could see clearly in the mirror, conveyed impatience or a kind of satisfaction.

The park was buzzing. People were picnicking, playing frisbee, sun tanning and doing anything and everything that people do to pass the time relaxing on a beautiful August day. I changed in the car and joined the girls, who had stretched out on a large blanket, not far from the pond. They'd stripped down to their bikini tops: pink for Vicky and white for Jessie. I started warming up on the grass but I couldn't keep myself from eyeing them as they lay there on their blanket.

They were talking quietly between themselves. I could hear Jessie clearly enough, in spite of the fact she was whispering. But it was impossible to hear Vicky.

I was about to take off running when Vicky shook a bottle of sunscreen in my direction.

"He's Innu!" quickly exclaimed Jessie. A rapid exchange of glances took place between Vicky and me. Jessie must have realized she wasn't getting the whole picture. The keenness with which she had jumped in told me all I needed to know. I let them know that my mother was Québécoise and that even Innu didn't spend the whole day in the sun unless they wanted to burn like anybody else. I took the bottle out of Vicky's hand.

Our fingers brushed. I couldn't tell if she did it on purpose.

I slathered sunscreen over my arms and shoulders. Now it was the girls who were discreetly watching me out of the corners of their eyes. After thanking Vicky, I gave them both a wave and took off on the run.

In my mind, I could hear Larry's voice:

"You're a power forward, Alex, never forget it."

The day was gorgeous. The ducks were quacking. A group of African Quebecers were chilling, listening to dubstep. Some guy in a Chevy Nova laid rubber, sending up a cloud of smoke and perfuming the air with the aroma of burnt tires. And all along the bike path, the dance of families on their two-wheelers enjoying the extraordinary weather. Summers are short, winters are long, and people try desperately to extract as much pleasure as they can from a beautiful day, like squeezing the last drop from an old lemon.

My legs were solid and my pulse was steady. On the other hand, I was having a hard time getting my wind. It was hot and I was drenched with sweat. It ran down my face and into my eyes. I might have been pushing it a little too much for the heat of the day, like somebody in too much of a hurry to get where he's going. The most important thing in running is to find a steady pace. But the scent of the sunscreen kept reminding me of Jessie and Vicky. I wondered what that loser Tommy was doing. He was probably at the back of the gym pumping big iron and getting shots of dope in his bum. Funny... Not even a year ago, he'd have been the one hanging out with the prettiest girls in town while I'd be cruising alone in my quad in the sand pit beside the municipal garbage dump.

When I came back to near the duck pond, Vicky was all alone. I let myself drop to her side, catching my breath. When I asked her where Jessie was, she answered by shaking her water bottle in the direction of the drinking fountain. There she was, in the distance, holding two bottles of water, talking with some people.

"You don't say very much, do you?" I asked. I could sense her looking me up and down from behind her sunglasses. Her navel was filled with the same sweat that was trickling down her long slender frame.

"What are you doing tomorrow night?" she asked.

Finally, I heard her speak. Her voice was deep, with a slight tremolo. And something nasal as well, but incredibly seductive. In fact, even if she had sounded like a gorilla, I would have found her cute. I was bitten.

Before I could say anything at all, she added, in all directness and with little modesty:

"My mom's spending the night at her boyfriend's tomorrow. She'll be back late. Do you want to see me?"

I felt my legs go wobbly. And the butterflies in my stomach. The sun was burning me and the dubstep pounding from across the park made my head spin.

Jessie returned, walking barefoot on the grass. When she noticed me watching her, she waved hello, flashing me a big smile. Discreetly, I palmed the piece of paper that Vicky scooted across the blanket. On it was her phone number, written in pink.

"I figured you'd be pretty thirsty," said Jessie, kneeling beside me.

She was breathtakingly beautiful. I held the piece of paper in my fist, squeezing it like a school kid afraid to be found out in class. On full breakaway, a good hockey player has to rely on his instincts more than anything else. That gives him a clear advantage over his opponents. He has to move for the best opening without a second thought. That was the mark of a champion.

I thanked her in all sincerity, telling her how thoughtful I thought she was. Then, I drank two-thirds of the bottle before sinking back down on the blanket, one arm shielding my face from the sun. Jessie was lying on my left, Vicky stretched out on my right. I could feel each of their thighs touching my own.

We stayed like that for close to half an hour. Until, totally fried by the sun, we couldn't take any more and got up to look for some shade. Vicky was waiting in the car, the radio cranked all the way up, as if she didn't really want to hear what Jessie was saying to me. Jessie had taken me by the hand to hold me back. She wanted to talk to me. Under the shade of a big tree, on the sidewalk, she asked me what I was doing later on. I was busy, I told her. Then I kissed her on the cheek, saying I was glad to have seen her. I watched her climb into the car, and I started running again, pretty sure I'd seen Vicky flash me a huge grin in the rear-view mirror.

I ran down the cycling path and then over the iron bridge. After passing through the industrial park, I crossed an overpass that brought me close to the baseball stadium. I took the back streets back to my apartment.

Something potent, primordial energy was driving me on. This time, it wasn't fear that sent my feet flying; it was desire. My strides, normally heavy and regular, were light and nimble, carrying me along at full speed. I felt something akin to hunger. That was it. I was hungry. There was a taste in my mouth. It wasn't fresh like hay or putrid like lake algae. It was blood. My mouth was wide open, dripping with saliva, my teeth long and sharp. I paused at every corner, sniffing the air, alert, looking all around, with the irresistible urge to call out to the pack to follow me.

Back at the apartment, Larry was in a fine mood. Which was a relief, considering what I'd discovered in his closet. I'd been holding my breath, afraid I'd find him sitting on the couch with his arms folded behind his head and the gun on the coffee table, asking me if I was the one who'd been going through his stuff. Instead, a chef's apron tied around his waist, he ushered me into the kitchen where he was in the midst of preparing two humungous T-bones fresh from the butcher.

When he saw me, he let out a whoop, saying how glad he was to see me. He offered me a beer that I gingerly nursed, a little suspicious of the whole setup. Larry wasn't the kind of guy to offer you a beer, usually. He was more likely to whip up a banana smoothie, loaded with protein powder.

"So," he asked. "how'd it go?"

"Great."

"What do you think?"

"I made the cut, for sure."

"You can say it again, for sure!" he said, slapping me on the back with one hand as he held the steaks on a wooden cutting board in the other.

Out in Nathalie's back yard, the table was set with placemats, plates and condiments. Smoke billowed out of the gas grill along with the smell of grilled onions. I glanced up towards the house; the door was shut and the window curtains were closed.

"Don't worry, she's away for a few days. Nobody to get on our case."

So that explained his good mood and the impromptu little party.

It was just what I needed, this dinner for two. I'd piled up more than my share of unpleasant moments since I'd arrived in town. Me too, I felt like celebrating. Camp was going smoothly, I'd just come back from a great afternoon and Vicky's phone number was in my pocket.

Larry put the steaks on the grill and I sat down at the table, enjoying the scent of the flowers in Nathalie's garden.

"What's on your mind, big guy?" said Larry, dishing me up the big T-bone, which began to swim in its juices.

"Nothing much," I said.

He heaped my plate with grilled onions and a baked potato that had been cooking in the blood-red sauce. I was hungry. We talked about hockey and whatever else came into our minds while we ate. Larry was upbeat and talkative. Too talkative.

He spoke passionately of the Côte-Nord: of its beautiful and extraordinary land. Of spaces so vast that you could get lost forever and never be found. He remembered going fishing with his uncle Henri when he was a kid: maybe he should go back to sea. Crab fishing was hard work, he knew. But he was tired of lousy low-paying jobs. He didn't have any illusions. He realized he'd never make a good coach and would never go any higher than midgets. He dreamed of buying his own place somewhere between Sept-Îles and Havre-Saint-Pierre, maybe at Rivière-au-Tonnerre or Magpie. With any luck, he'd pick up something cheap right on the water. He was tired of being a loser who lived in a semi-basement in the middle of some town. For the first time in his life, he had something to live for. He could feel it: the taste of freedom.

It made me really happy to see him like that. I'd only been half tuned in as he blabbered on, his little eyes sparkling, his gestures excessive, too expressive, like an Italian mamma. Slouched on my patio chair, feeling the beer, I floated in a sea of blond hair, gold as honey, and the alluring scent of goddesses.

"Alex, I'm leaving tomorrow."

And with that, I stopped daydreaming and sat bolt upright in my chair. Larry had said a lot of things, jumping from one subject to another, idealizing life and dreaming of a better future. I knew they were only dreams. I couldn't believe he was set on making them come true, certainly not any time soon.

"Are you serious?"

"Totally."

"But rookie camp ends tomorrow. Real camp starts next week. Don't you want to see how I make out with the older guys?"

He smiled, shaking his head from left to right.

"It's obvious you don't need me anymore, Alex. I've been watching how you handle yourself. You've done amazing. A hell of a lot better than I ever imagined. I talked to your coach. It's in the bag, believe me. Starting next week, he's putting you on a line with Steven Caron and Ruslan Abishkin. He says you'll be turning heads this season. Do you know what that means? If it happens, if you end up Abishkin's right winger, you've got a good shot at winning rookie of the year. That just about guarantees you'll be first NHL draft pick."

He was exaggerating about a top draft pick. Not too many players from Quebec had gone high in the draft in recent years. But what was even more striking was that I had never, ever, heard Larry say anything like that about me before. His style was to bring me down to earth by telling me I wasn't good enough, I wasn't working hard enough.

I must say I was disappointed, even a little sad, to hear him. His confession and all the compliments seemed to be saying that he wouldn't be my coach any more, that he was letting me go.

And still he went on: "Your skating is way above average. You're tall and agile. You've got great range. An accurate shot, really amazing!"

Night was falling on the city with a coolness that soothed my sunburned skin. I could hear the distant siren of a police car and the cries of children playing in the park. Then Larry began to speak about love. A love that was deeper and stronger than anything else.

"Love, McKenzie. That's all that matters."

I thought he wanted to get his life together because he had met a girl. Probably on one of those Internet dating sites he hung out on.

The next day was the cut. Practice got going with some on-ice skill exercises, but it was mostly an informal skate, more informative than anything else. What was left to evaluate? I didn't know. Everything had been said and demonstrated over the previous days. Maybe they wanted a last chance to evaluate the character of some unidentified prospects who had shown perseverance and hard work. So these guys who never quit could be called up in case there were too many injuries over the season.

One by one, we met with the coach in his office. I went first. While I was pretty sure I'd made it, especially after what Larry told me, nothing was one hundred percent sure. Rookie camp, apart from some rough spots with Tommy, had seemed almost too easy. As I entered the coach's office, I suddenly wondered if perhaps I had been wrong all along. Maybe the coaches hadn't said anything to me during camp because I really sucked. Larry, who'd been a little weird for a while, could say just about anything. And I was well aware that my gut feelings, my convictions, didn't count for much. Since, in general, nothing ever happened the way I expected.

My evaluation was positive, except that I was criticized for playing the pass too often and not supporting my teammates enough on defence. I demonstrated good conditioning aptitudes, but I had a tendency to fall asleep when the tempo of the game slowed. I had to stay alert. I admit that I often play the long pass. That had been my role in recent years. And I had wanted to show them that I could score goals, which I did. Larry had given me more than my share of lectures over the past year on the same subject: my lack of heart.

The coach, who had been a star in the NHL, congratulated me in any case and said he saw no problem in my making the team. But he wanted more intensity. And if he didn't get it, he wouldn't hesitate to send me down to midgets. I immediately replied that he could count on me, which was what he wanted to hear.

"The problem with talented guys like you is that you tend to forget that you have a lot to learn before you move up. Next week you'll start skating with guys who are older and stronger. Guys who've been with us for one, two and even three years. Guys who have one thing in mind: not getting beat out by someone younger. It'll be, I think, the first real test in your young career. What you'll learn during the coming weeks will serve you the rest of your life."

"Got it."

"So we'll see you next week."

We shook hands, as if we were signing a contract. The "Larry" years were already behind me. It was a new beginning, one that filled me with optimism.

Big tall Danny from Rouyn-Noranda came after me. Then, a defenceman named Michaud, a guy who liked making noises with his mouth and who stood six feet four inches tall. Then came Tommy and the rest.

I passed by them, saying nothing, and continued my way down the corridor with my hands in my pockets. I didn't meet anybody's eye, I didn't smile. I might have even looked worried. I know it worried them. If I—who had been hands down the best player in the camp—was leaving my evaluation with a look like that on my face, what was in store for them?

Tommy had to suffer through some long minutes of waiting. He sat on the bench, body leaning forward, elbows on his thighs. He remained motionless, his eyes on the black rubber carpet at his feet. He muttered as if he was praying, begging God to give him his chance. He was drenched in sweat. His ears and neck were red, just like during the first day of camp. Tommy, unable to rely on his talent, had decided to rely on his tough guy capabilities, and he had every reason to be anxious.

When I stepped into the locker room, a reporter came up to me, asking me how I felt. I was surprised that the team had informed him about my selection before they'd spoken to me. When I asked him, he said it was just a hunch. In his years covering hockey, he'd seen a lot of guys get cut. And he just had a feeling I wasn't going to be one of them. I replied that I was very happy, relieved even. But I had my work cut out for me. I definitely had to keep at it because the hardest part was still ahead. The important thing was to do my best and take advantage of every opportunity that came along.

It was like I'd rehearsed my answers. All the hockey interviews I'd watched over the years must have conditioned me to give stock answers.

In a good mood and without a care in the world, I thought I'd pull on my skates and hit the ice. That seemed like the perfect way to enjoy this moment of intense happiness. I stepped onto the ice in my street clothes, equipped only with my skates, gloves and stick. The ice was empty and the stands were completely deserted. The big lights that hung from the Colisée's roof were turned down low, and the ice was dark and grey.

"You've got to get off in an hour," I was told by the equipment manager. "The crew's showing up at one o'clock. They have to put up a great big stage, there's a concert in two days."

And, before the ice got covered with black plywood panels and a bunch of storage containers on wheels, I started skating with long, slow thrusts, hugging the boards.

I circled the ice effortlessly, slowly, with my eyes closed. I've always loved skating with my eyes closed when I'm alone on the ice. I let my instincts take over and play with balancing my sense of the space with the strength and rhythm of my movements. I had to have total faith in my own abilities. You pay for it when it doesn't work. But when it works, and your coordination is perfect, it's great. I still hadn't opened my eyes after three full laps. In my mind's eye, I could clearly see the ice and the crowd. The Colisée was packed and cheering as one for a goal I had just drilled off the curve of my stick after a dramatic breakaway. I came quickly back to earth when I heard the door to the team bench close with a bang. I put on the brakes and opened my eyes. It was Tommy.

True to himself and with his usual zeal, he had come alone to put in his after-practice workout. He jumped on the ice and upended a plastic tub with a blow from his stick, tumbling a dozen pucks onto the ice.

He was decked out in full gear which, combined with a muscle mass out of the ordinary, made him look like a gladiator. I don't know why, but I felt uneasy. Maybe because I only had on light cotton clothes and the ice suddenly seemed threatening. He gave three or four thrusts of his blades and then let himself glide for a long moment, leaning forward, his stick resting on his knees.

All of a sudden, he exploded towards the pucks that had rolled into the middle of the faceoff circle. He jammed on the brakes, sending a cloud of snow into the air. Then, gathering all his momentum and with a cry of rage, he drilled a puck right at me. It struck the boards behind me with a mighty *thwap* that resonated through-out the Colisée. If I hadn't lifted my leg at the very last moment, it would have hit me right on my knee.

"Hey, you fucking idiot!" I cried. "Are you totally nuts?"

He stood still and didn't say a thing. I couldn't make out his face through his visor, but I could imagine, or even feel, his dark look. He toyed with a puck in front of him.

"Hey, you big schizoid!" I continued. "I'm talking to you!"

And he was at it again, striking all three pucks with all his strength, which I dodged.

There was no getting out of it. He was doing it on purpose. He was provoking me, and I wasn't going to take it. I threw my gloves down and skated towards him, rolling up the sleeves of my sweatshirt. He threw down his own gloves and tore off his helmet. He backed up slowly, giving me the "come here" signal. He smiled nastily. His acne-covered face was red and dripping with sweat. Scary.

"Come on, McKenzie, let's go! Let's go!"

I went.

I'd been well trained for the game of hockey. But I was completely useless at fighting. And for sure Tommy's training program with his cousin from Baie-Comeau and Vincent included a number of the techniques used by goons. Tommy picked me up by my collar and sent two punches right into my face that I couldn't counter. My knees gave out and I'd certainly have fallen if he, with his powerful arms, hadn't held me up. I pathetically tried to hit back, but without success. Seeing that he was about to punch me in the face again, I ducked my head and took it right in the nuts. Unable to protect myself from the avalanche of blows that followed, I let myself fall to the ice.

He had me by my neck and was rubbing my face into the ice.

"What's up, you big asshole?" I shouted angrily. "You didn't have a good evaluation?"

"I haven't even had my evaluation!" he said, bringing his face close to mine. "They made me pee in a bottle. If my test is positive, they're sending me home. And if that happens, McKenzie, you'd better watch out. Because I promise you that you're going back to the Côte-Nord same as me. But in a coffin! Got it?"

I didn't respond.

"Got it?!" he shouted, this time.

"Go fuck yourself, Tom! You're a fucking moron!"

Furious, he smacked my head three or four times against the ice before moving away, skating backwards. I looked up, blood dripping down my face. My eyebrow was cut and it was bleeding profusely. I just couldn't believe that Larry would have said a word about all that to the coach. I knew I hadn't told anyone what I'd seen in the basement of the gym.

Tommy, laughing, shot a couple of pucks at me. Kneeling at centre ice, I couldn't avoid them, and they hit me hard. They weren't hard shots. It was just to taunt me. Any way you take it though, a frozen puck doesn't feel very good.

Curled up on the ice, I waited until he left before I lifted my head. When I left the rink, the technicians were coming in with plywood panels mounted on trolleys. They were building the stage for the show. They watched me go by without commenting, my face full of blood, as if they were seeing an apparition: a ghost from the old days when the Canadiens fought the Nordiques.

◉

I took a taxi home. I had a bandage covering my right eyebrow. The wound was neither serious nor deep. Still, a cut on the brow bone bleeds. When the taxi dropped me off, I saw Larry's Jeep parked on the sidewalk in front of the park. All four flashers were blinking. The retractable roof was rolled back and I could see his bags in the back. He was ready to go and that was fine with me. I had had just about enough of him. But I was glad to catch him before he left. Because I had a few words to say to him.

I walked into the apartment like a man on fire and made straight for his room. I found him sitting on his bed, one hand in his leather jacket. I immediately thought of the revolver and I stepped back into the doorway. He seemed relieved that it was me and pulled his hand from his jacket.

There was a whiff of perfume in his room. His red hair was wet and combed to the side. Besides his leather jacket, he had on a pair of brand new jeans and white tennis shoes. He looked confused.

"What are you doing here? Aren't you supposed to be at practice?"

"No, Larry. Rookie camp's over, remember? We had evaluations today."

"Did you make the team?"

"You bet I made the team, what did you think?"

"And Tom?"

I could have punched him right in the mouth. I took a deep breath, but couldn't even get a word out. I felt a presence to my left. I turned my head slightly and saw in the corner of the room, behind the old yellow armchair, a little girl watching me, her hands resting on the back of the chair.

She had a full head of red hair that fell pell-mell over her shoulders. On her white sweater, a silver star pulled a multi-coloured rainbow in its wake. She froze. The way she was looking at me made me immediately uncomfortable. It wasn't a look of fear or amazement; it was one of defiance. Her tiny steel-blue eyes looking straight through me, there was no doubt who she was. Larry's daughter, Melissa.

Incredulous, I raised my hands in front of me, shaking my head from left to right. As I was about to express my dismay, Larry lifted his index finger to silence me. The girl, who must have been about ten, darted toward him. She clung to his arm, never taking her accusatory eyes off me. Larry was also staring at me. But it was a tender look, like that of a wise man or a priest. He gently nodded his head as he would have done in the face of a great truth.

"Love, McKenzie. Love! That's all that counts. It's stronger than anything. Stronger than justice, judges and all the inhuman machinery that governs our sick society. When nonsense takes over and we no longer know what to do, what to say, how to act, there's one thing that should count, and that's love. It's the end point of all reason, McKenzie. The light at the end of the tunnel. Otherwise, there's nothing left. And that's unacceptable to any free man!"

Larry spoke with calm conviction, reciting his speech as he would have done in the dressing room between the second and third periods of game seven in the play-offs. I tried as hard as I could to keep a cool head and not to get caught up in his psycho's mumbo-jumbo. I had to find a way to pop this "bubble" which, carried by a powerful wind, was leading him far from the reason he claimed as his guide.

"Uh ... listen, Larry, I understand what you're trying to say. But your daughter. Did you think about her? Because it's all about her, isn't it?"

And the answer came quickly. But it didn't come from him. But rather from his daughter, who sat up on the bed and looked at me as would a cat that you were about to plunge into a cold bath, legs rigged, back arched, hair on end and claws extended.

"I'm staying with my daddy!"

It was as if her tiny cold and bloodshot eyes were about to overflow with repressed anger, about to explode. I was walking on eggshells with this little person. It was a look that I had come to know very well during my previous hockey seasons. It was scary Larry. Scary Larry who had fought in the Balkans and who had incessantly goaded me to push beyond my limits. The kind of look that makes you run barefoot on the sand and climb the dunes under a blazing sun.

Larry stroked his daughter's head and kissed her on the forehead. She folded into her father's hug without taking her eyes off me, as if responding to a supreme challenge to their moment of intimacy, as if she was telling me, "If you ever try to take me away from him, I'll rip your heart out!"

"Love, McKenzie," he added, like a litany or a mantra which seemed to occupy his entire mind. "It's only love that matters. From now on, nothing else interests me."

He stood up, taking her by the hand. They brushed past me and I stepped aside to let them pass.

"Larry, I don't think your plan's going to work. The cops will be on your tail in no time."

"It doesn't matter how it all turns out, McKenzie. What's important is that my conscience is clear."

And they left, closing the door behind them, leaving me in the cold and lifeless living room.

I should have let them go, and good riddance. What in the world was Larry thinking? That he would roll all the way to the Côte-Nord like some kind of desperado, in his Jeep with the police in hot pursuit, shooting at them with his revolver? It wouldn't take the provincial police even an hour to catch up with him. There's only one road home. And a Jeep with a lynx airbrushed on its hood is not exactly a stealth machine.

I heard the engine start up outside. He gunned it a couple of times and put it in gear. The Jeep rolled slowly past the living room window. Impulsively, acting purely on instinct, I dashed out the door running at full tilt down Rue du Roi towards the 4 x 4 that had stopped for a light at the next intersection. Larry saw me coming in the rear-view mirror. He took off before the light turned green. Brakes squealed. He barely missed the mail truck that drove by in front of him, leaning on its horn, bringing him to a panic stop right in the middle of the street. There was a chorus of honking from drivers who were pissed off at such a clueless idiot. That gave me all the time I needed to grab hold of the roll bar and lift myself into the rear of the vehicle. I ended up in the back seat, between the bags.

Larry, hemmed in on all sides, had no choice but to move forward to get out of his predicament. He drove slowly to the next red light, furious.

"McKenzie, get out!"

"No way, Larry. I'm not getting out. You're doing something that's wicked crazy, man."

"If you don't get out right this minute, it's going to get nasty."

He turned onto Boulevard Charest, which led to the Montmorency Expressway. If he could of, he would have stopped to put a judo move on me and toss me out of the Jeep. But there were police sirens screaming all over the city. And that made him extremely nervous. He'd have been nervous for less. He had no reason to think they weren't coming after him. Melissa hadn't returned to class after recess. They'd seen her father hanging around the schoolyard a few days earlier. But now the row of green lights that extended one after the other all the way to the on ramp were an opportunity he couldn't afford to pass up. With better things to think about than me, he rammed the pedal to the floor and we took off at full speed, the powerful engine humming under the hood.

Once on the highway towards Beauport Bay, he began to bawl me out.

"First chance I get, Alex, I'm pulling over and you're getting out."

"No way, Larry. You've totally lost it. We're a team, remember? I'm not leaving you alone. You're about to make the worst mistake of your whole life."

"The worst mistake of my whole life is to have wasted my time coaching you instead of being close to my daughter!"

I wanted to tell him that it was out of love for him, my completely dysfunctional coach, that I was right there by his side. It was thanks to Larry, who had known me since I was in bantams, that I had come as far as I had. It was he who'd convinced my father, repeating it over and over that I had what it took to be one of the best. He'd had to push me not to quit, because I was incorrigibly lazy. And now, with my future in my own hands, I jump headlong into extended workouts that I really enjoy, and nobody has to tell me to do it. I owed him a lot. And if he had to go off the deep end, I was ready to go with him. That was probably an example of the kind of dead-end reasoning that he just talked about a little earlier.

With the wind in my face, I yelled:

"Do you know how to straighten out nonsense, Larry? Eh?"

He glowered at me in the rear-view. I was pretty sure we'd be getting back to the subject at some later date, and when we did, he was going to thank me.

The Jeep sped along the highway at over 160 km/hr. The St. Lawrence was on my right and the easternmost tip of Île d'Orléans came in and out of view through a light fog. Ahead, a ship lay at anchor. The brown waters of Beauport Bay were still. The sky was grey and heavy. Tiny droplets began falling. The roof was open and Larry cursed because he couldn't afford to stop and close it. We were soaked in no time.

And, far behind us, alongside the Daishowa mill, I saw the flashing lights of the police hot on our tail. When I mentioned it to Larry, he nodded nervously. He'd spotted them too. Maybe he was hoping to make it to Charlevoix, where, in his delirium, he might have been able to find a place to hide. But, there on Boulevard Sainte-Anne, between the river and the Côte-de-Beaupré, he was trapped.

His grip on the steering wheel became less and less assured. And the Jeep, running at full speed, swerved dangerously out of its lane several times. Again and again he ran his hand through his hair, swivelling his head from left to right, chest scrunched up against the steering wheel as if he was looking for something.

The little girl didn't seem to be worried about anything much except me. She glared at me with an uncommon intensity typical of children. Something more animal than human. It seemed as though she had waited all her life to live this crazy cartoon where her father, the knight in shining armour, comes riding in to rescue her from all her troubles. She'd always known that the great hockey coach would one day come to find her. Well, that day had finally come. And I was the spanner in the works. The guy threatening to demolish the beautiful plans her father had dangled in front of her eyes.

I would have liked to tell her that it was just a fantasy, that it wasn't going to have a happy ending, that life didn't work out that way. But it wouldn't have done any good. And anyway, I couldn't bring myself to do it. There are looks that are so sincere, so uncompromising, that you can't do anything but bow your head and keep your mouth shut. Little Melissa terrified me.

The cop cars had narrowed the gap but weren't coming too close, keeping a safe distance. There was a child in the car. Nobody wanted any injuries, not to mention any deaths. I figured it out: they were simply giving us escort until we were forced to pull over, one way or another.

"How far can you go on a tank of gas?' I asked.

"Theoretically, I should be able to make it to Baie-Comeau."

"And then what?"

About "then what" he had nothing to say. I wanted to ask if he was planning to fly across the Saguenay River, but there'd have been no point. It was starting to dawn on him that the game was over. He smiled half-heartedly, as if to tell Melissa that everything was going to be all right, but she wasn't fooled. His eyes were full of love as he looked at her and I knew that however this ended, there was no way he'd ever let any harm come to her.

A police helicopter had appeared over our heads, following us on the right. I was afraid for a moment that they'd open fire. But it turned out the guy I saw aiming something at us was just a cameraman. Larry kept a hand on his jacket as if feeling for the revolver through the leather. There was no way he could bring down the copter with one hand on the wheel.

The helicopter flew over our heads two or three times, backfiring. We passed through the town of Sainte-Anne-de-Beaupré with no cars in front of us and no oncoming traffic. The entire road had been closed so that we could pass without incident while the pursuit continued. Uniformed officers on both sides of the road and in the parking spaces in front of the stores made updates on our progress into their walkie-talkies. We were obviously surrounded with no way out. Operation "Melissa, mon amour" was a dismal failure.

"Bravo, Larry," I said, giving him a few pats on the shoulder. "You succeeded."

"Umm, I don't know," he said, adjusting his smoky blue sunglasses on his nose. "I'll probably make the papers. At least that's something."

Coming at such a critical moment, his quick flash of humour led me to believe he was going to surrender and all we'd have to suffer would be a good scare. But that was a wrong read on "Crazy Larry." The ending was going to have to be something spectacular. After discovering that the police had blocked the bridge over the Sainte-Anne River, he turned off to the right and started weaving through the maze of small residential streets, finally arriving at the road to Cap Tourmente.

The rain was falling in sheets. We were soaked from head to toe. Even if we had managed to ditch some of the police cars on the gravel road, the helicopter kept us always in its sights. After driving down the dirt road to the wildlife reserve, Larry swung onto a trail that led right down to the shore of the mighty St. Lawrence.

The full power of the Jeep, urged on by Larry's heavy foot, tore into the muddy trail. The helicopter pulled closer. The tall strands of yellow and green grass bobbed and rippled under the wind whipped up by the rotor and propellers. We splashed through the shallow pools sending water and mud flying. Hundreds of birds took to the air and the few tourists who were observing the wildlife from observation posts were no doubt wondering why.

We were getting dangerously close to the river. The Jeep, as powerful as it was, eventually bogged down in the increasingly wide and deep marshes. Larry spun his wheels backwards and forwards, churning up huge quantities of mud. But there was nothing else he could do. We were completely stuck.

The helicopter flew low over our heads. Hand in hand, Larry and Melissa jumped down from the Jeep and started running through the tall grass under the rain, towards majestic Cap Tourmente.

Leaving their cars at the end of the road, the police had started off in full pursuit. I thought it judicious to stay in the vehicle and not to try to do anything more. Rapidly, three officers surrounded the jeep, guns drawn, gesturing for me to get out. Which I did, putting my hands behind my head. They immediately jumped on me, pushing my face into the mud. They handcuffed me, yanking on the cuffs until they were as tight as they could go. I told them they were too tight, but their only response was a string of violent insults.

Larry and his daughter ran on in desperation, until, surrounded by a number of policemen, they fell to the grass. Larry, lying on his back, sank slowly into the wet mud while Melissa clung to him as hard as she could. In a tight embrace, the little girl finally understood what was happening and nestled her face one last time against her father's ear. She whispered to Larry, who had never been happier: "I love you forever, papa."

Chapter 6

Larry was right. He made the front pages of all the news-papers. His photo ran under the headline "Child Kid-napper." The close-up told the story: a guy in sunglasses with a receding hairline and tight little unsmiling lips. The perfect bastard. It was easy to hate him. All the major dailies ran pictures of the chase, taken from the helicopter. The most disturbing one showed him lying on the grass with Melissa, surrounded by cops.

As for me, the picture of me taken a week earlier by the journalist from *Le Soleil* was featured on page two. If Larry came off as the lowest of the low, I was a hero. The neighbours claimed they saw me running after the Jeep. After some pretty heavy questioning during which I laid out my version of the events, confirmed by Larry who swore he'd acted alone, the police finally released me. But the investigation would continue, they said; they'd be calling me back to answer more questions.

They'd decided to release me earlier, but they were waiting for my father to arrive before letting me go. Sylvie and Mike heard the news about 5:15 p.m. But by the time they'd located Louis in the woods it was past eight when they finally hit the road. They arrived at the Victoria Park police station around two in the morning. I was all alone in the large cell reserved for minors.

A tall policeman with a shaved head came to escort me out. He flashed me a big smile and gave me a pat on the back to cheer me up. Me, I was drained after my long day. The interrogation that evening had been difficult, with guys trying to pin me down on the specifics: Where was I at such and such a time, at such and such a moment, with whom, etc., even suggesting that maybe I was Larry's accomplice. I probably looked as bad as I felt, discouragement written all over my face. And the duty officer tried to reassure me: my ordeal was almost over, not to worry, everything was going to work out. The TV news, sensational as usual, featured me at the top of the hour as the guy who had bravely jumped into the Jeep in the middle of Boulevard Dorchester to try to reason with the maniac. I fully deserved everybody's gratitude.

Louis gave me a great big hug. So did Sylvie. Emotions were running high. Of course, the Smith & Wesson .357 Magnum Larry was packing when he was finally apprehended had been mentioned over and over on the news. As they'd driven in the pickup along the near-deserted road to Quebec City, they kept hearing the story on the radio, and each new detail pushed their stress off the dial.

The team sprung for a lawyer I was to meet the next morning. I spoke to him on the phone and he advised me not to say anything. If need be, they would call a press conference. Still, as we came out of the police station at three in the morning, two feature reporters followed me out to Louis's pickup asking questions. I answered as well as I could.

The next day, the lawyer let me have it. When the reporters had asked me my opinion of what Larry had done, I said it was wrong. When they'd asked me what I thought of him, I couldn't help saying he was a good guy and I liked him a lot. Grey areas don't really exist in newspapers. On the other hand, nothing in life is totally black or totally white. But headlines are always in boldface. And my statement was bound to raise more than a few eyebrows. The next day, in large type next to my bewildered face: "He's a good guy."

We spent the day at a hotel. After checking in around five in the morning, I went right to bed and slept soundly. When I awoke, I was alone with Sylvie. Louis had gone to get my things from Nathalie's and move them to my aunt's friend's place in Charlesbourg. And just like that, my life in the Basse-Ville came to an end. I was going to be living in a basement flat on Rue des Sureaux.

Vicky tried to reach me at Nathalie's a couple of times, but I never called her back. The whole episode with Larry had shaken me. And throughout my ordeal in the jail cell and with the hard-nosed police interrogator, the only person I could think about that brought me any comfort was Chloé. If I could only be in her arms and forget about everything.

I hadn't seen her since I left. She never made it to Quebec City, for all kinds of reasons. But she sent me a beautiful letter, together with some pictures. She said she'd gone up to my cabin a couple of times. There was a picture of her wearing a scarf on her head and a green fleece jacket, sitting on the steps. She wrote that when she smelled fir resin, she thought of me. Another photo showed her in Mike's garage. She was perched on my Skiroule holding his new dog: another husky, a male this time. His name was Amarok, which means "wolf" in Inuktitut. His hands dirty, the damn Bruins cap on his head, Michel had just finished making sure the snowmobile was ready for winter. In another shot, taken at arm's length, Chloé had taken a picture of herself with the sea in the background. The sky was grey. Her eyes were closed. She had a big smile, and her wet hair hung down over her face.

A couple of news photographers started snapping their cameras at me Monday morning when I arrived at the official opening of training camp. It was kind of weird for a rookie to be getting all that attention.

My father and I met with the coach before practice. It was all very informal. We joked around. He told us there was absolutely no reason not to start camp at the same time as everybody else. I should concentrate on my game, he said; he was used to controversy and that the media would forget the story in about twenty-four hours. That was a news story's life cycle. Hero or zero.

"A strange sort of a bird," he said of Larry. "He came to see me a couple of times. He wasn't the easiest guy to follow."

"He's a bit too intense," said Louis, as if he was at confession. "He just lost it."

My father had always liked Larry and what happened had really upset him. More than anything else, he felt embarrassed, as if he had to apologize for entrusting me to a guy like that. I would have liked to stop him, to convince him that it wasn't worth it, but I couldn't. And now, every time I defended Larry the least little bit, people looked at me with raised eyebrows. The way they condemned Larry shocked me more than a little.

I was about to meet my teammates for the first time. All eyes were on me and you could hear a pin drop as I came into the locker room. A guy named Plaisance cracked a joke and there were a few guffaws. I shrugged and said nothing.

In a minute, the hubbub level you find in a veteran locker room was back to normal. The guys had already known each other for a couple of years. They were back for another season with a single clear ambition: to make the grade as professionals. Either in the ECHL, the AHL or, best of all, the NHL. Danny was the first to come up to me and shake my hand.

"Wow, man. I was watching it live. It was amazing!"

I guess it was.

Among the newcomers, besides Danny and me, there was the friendly giant, Michaud. And in a corner, talking loudly with some of the veterans, Tommy. I was surprised to see him. With all the performance enhancers he'd been taking, I expected him to flunk the lab test and find himself on the first bus home. But apparently not. There he was, pulling on his skates with an ear-splitting grin. He even said Hi to me.

Good for him, I said to myself. Maybe what he was taking was perfectly legal. Protein injections? What did I know? With all the new discoveries in sports medicine, anything was possible. What bothered me though, was the way he kept running Larry down. He'd tell anyone who'd listen that he knew Larry pretty well, and he'd always thought there was something strange about him. That was why he'd refused to train with him this summer. And also why he'd wanted to get away from him by moving out of the apartment on Rue du Roi. He seemed to be inferring that Larry had been propositioning him. What nerve!

It was a story made to measure for a pathological liar like Tommy. He could use it to conceal his cheating and to soothe his conscience. Because that's what's hardest for a cheater, his conscience. It's always there, reminding him of his dishonesty. He grabs at any opportunity to justify himself, to make himself feel more righteous. That was why he wasn't missing a chance to describe Larry as a dangerous sicko.

We jumped onto the ice to warm up. Half an hour of continuous skating helps you get focused. At one point, while we were circling the ice as if on a giant carousel, I caught up to Tommy, who was skating faster than everybody else, like a madman.

"They decided to keep you after all?" I tossed out.

"Were you afraid they wouldn't?" he shot back.

And took off with a vengeance, as if he had a rocket in his bum.

He had promised I'd go home in a coffin if he tested positive. It would take an inquest to demonstrate the extent of the authorities' negligence. The fact that they'd taken a sample of his urine indicated that some kind of a proceeding had been initiated. There was every reason to believe that it was actually Larry who had gotten the ball rolling. Doping controls are very sporadic in hockey and virtually non-existent during the off-season. But after Larry was guilty of kidnapping his own daughter, the case was apparently shelved, or at least was never submitted to the Canadian Centre for Ethics in Sport, which handles such offenses. How could you take the ravings of a lunatic seriously? The sample never showed up anywhere. Or at least, someone, somewhere, had decided to look the other way.

Tommy had extraordinary physical abilities. Well above the average of the other guys on the team. While everybody else was paying attention to his own game, I kept my eye on him. I could tell he was in pain the previous week, after a training session. His face told the whole story. He was leaning on his stick, shifting his weight from one leg to the other. He was red and sweaty as usual, but I could see him clenching his teeth to hold back the pain that seemed to rise from his stomach and cause him to lean forward slightly every time his face twitched.

Here the level of play was very high. And for the first time since I arrived in Quebec City, I began to have doubts about my own abilities. I gave it everything I had, but the passes were coming hard on my stick and I made quite a few miscues. More than once, Carl had to tell me to settle down. But I couldn't help but feel intimidated by guys like Steven Caron and Ruslan Abishkin.

Steven Caron was one tough customer. He came from Maniwaki. He was the same height as me, but twice as strong. Of course, he was nineteen. He seemed laid back, kind of floating around, maybe a little oversized. But when he exploded, you'd better get out of the way. He could play the body and wasn't afraid of anyone: a real machine. Abishkin was cut from the same cloth. He wasn't as physical as Caron, but every bit as explosive. His skating was amazing. For anyone who's never tried to defend against someone like him, it'd be hard to imagine how the guy could change gears. First, second, third, fourth: he seemed to be accelerating: you would calculate your angle to intercept him and bang! He'd turn it up a notch and leave you in his wake. I got trapped a couple of times. He made me look like a pee-wee each and every time. I knew my father was cringing up in the stands.

I wasn't playing that well and feeling kind of down in the dumps about it but my accurate shooting saved the day. I figured that I was playing so poorly—coming in at the bottom in every area of play—that I might as well just relax. My shots were right on the net—even the team's starting goalie Loïc Martin couldn't believe it. Louis and Sylvie were standing on their seats, clapping and cheering to beat the band, as if they thought it might influence the coaches.

Carl slid me the puck; I was on top of it with one thrust of my skate and I placed it exactly where I wanted to.

"Hey, man? Where'd you learn to shoot like that?" asked one guy.

"Against the garage, back home."

In fact, from the time I could hold a hockey stick, I'd spent many a long day slapping pucks and tennis balls.

It had been a hard day for me, a reality check. I was far from out of the woods.

My father and aunt met me at the exit with all the usual encouragements. To hear them tell it, I had played well.

"Bravo! Really something to see how you hold your own with those guys."

But I wasn't fooled. I knew down deep that my day had been anything but outstanding. Still, I was confident that I'd be able to improve tomorrow.

"We invited Tommy to eat with us," said Louis.

"Oh?" I said.

That really surprised me. Above all that he agreed. Later, we were all sitting around the table at the Saint-Hubert BBQ on Boulevard Hamel. Nobody had much to say. There was tension in the air.

Tommy hadn't had a very good day, either. In fact, it had been a lot worse than mine. I'd at least pulled my chestnuts out of the fire with a few good shots whereas Tommy spent the day getting pummelled black and blue. Tommy never had chosen to hone his hockey skills, to go head to head with the best. He would compete with the tough guys. Not young talented prospects drafted out of the midgets and carefully groomed for success. Like me. The guys he was tangling with had no illusions: the only chance they had to make it in the pros was to be extremely intimidating and never give an opponent an inch. The difference between success and failure was tiny. And the blows could be vicious. A guy of sixteen was easy pickings. The goons and bullies had thrown themselves on Tom like lions on a piece of fresh meat.

But he gave as good as he got. He'd battled impres-
sively, even heroically, along the boards, getting cross-
checked from behind, each time getting back up with
fierce determination. But he was dead tired, and it
showed. He didn't want to be with us and had accepted
my father's invitation simply to be polite.

His forehead was twitching like before, his veins bulging. Several times I saw him clutching his stomach in
pain. He only ate half his chicken leg. He didn't seem
hungry. How could you not be hungry after a day like
we'd had?

His phone rang twice. Each time, I recognized the
voice of Vincent, the big bodybuilder. Tommy spoke to
him, turning away, not wanting us to overhear. But we
could hear everything well enough. The first time the
discussion was pretty calm.

"Yes, yes, yes," he repeated endlessly as if responding
to a long list of recommendations.

"It won't be long. I'm eating with some friends. People
from back home, don't worry."

He hung up and sighed, then continued toying
with his coleslaw. The second call was shorter. Vincent
had raised his voice, and I thought I could hear him
cursing.

"Listen Vince, I'm coming, it won't be long. You're
not going to lose a customer."

My father asked if he was in trouble. Tommy said no.

It was pouring rain. Sylvie and Louis ran out to the
parking lot and quickly climbed into the pickup. Tommy
and I lingered for a moment under the awning next to
the take-out window. He wanted to talk to me. Two

delivery-men came out with boxes of chicken stacked on top of one another.

"I need your help," he said.

"My help? For sure. What's going on?"

"I owe Vincent some money. I work for him. But, you know, I've got to quit. I can't handle it any more. It's not working out."

It was great news and a huge relief! I promised to support him and do whatever I could to help him get out of his tight spot and stop doping. I'd help him out for the rest of the camp. We'd work together, so that he could get it together before the season started.

"I need to move my things."

"Where are you going to stay?"

"I found an apartment."

"We can ask my father to come with the pickup."

"No. No family. Just you and me."

"Did you talk with your mother?"

"Yeah, I did. She's the one who found me the apartment. But don't tell anyone. You're the only one I can trust. Vincent scares me. My cousin in Baie-Comeau has started harassing my mother. It's big, Alex. You've got to keep it quiet. These guys aren't fooling around."

"Don't worry, bud. I'll help you."

We shook hands. Then we hugged. I wanted to leave, but he kept on holding me tight. When I managed to tear myself away, I saw him grimacing in pain. I felt sorry for him. I hoped his decision would change things for the better, and the whole nightmare would soon be over.

We took him home to a small street in Limoilou, near 2nd and 4th; the place looked a little scary. He lived on the ground floor of a real dump. The porch was falling apart and weeds had completely invaded the small piece of ground on either side.

As he stepped out of the car into the rain, he held the door open and said:

"So we'll be seeing each other later."

"I'll be there at eight on the dot." I jotted down his address on a piece of paper.

"What happens at eight?" asked Sylvie.

"Nothing. Chill, play some Xbox." Sylvie, usually a worry-wart, seemed relieved.

Louis insisted on driving me back, but I told him I'd take the bus. Besides, he was with Claude, Sylvie's girl-friend's boyfriend, and they'd drunk one too many. I took the Henri-Bourassa bus, which went down to 1st Avenue in Limoilou.

The rain had stopped. I walked, hands in my pockets, trying to remember where we'd left Tommy off a few hours earlier. The streets were confusing and I got lost. Finally, I recognized the big brick building and I turned down his street. Unsure, I climbed the rusty iron stairs. The concrete structure was disintegrating and the land-ing seemed to be suspended in thin air. I didn't have to knock. Tommy opened the door.

"Come in," he said, casting a glance up and down street as if he was afraid I'd been followed. Then he closed the door quickly behind me.

He lived in a huge six and a half room apartment. What was really troubling was that all the rooms were completely empty. In the kitchen there was a refrigerator and an old stove with a missing burner. There was a small room way at the back. It must have been his bed-room. A bare mattress was on the floor, no sheets or pillow. It was dusty and filthy. At the door sill lay a hockey bag and a suitcase. He was all set to leave this unhealthy environment that Vincent called home.

While Tommy was in the bathroom, I opened the fridge. Just some milk, three eggs, and some out-of-date hamburger that had turned brown. On the counter: three huge containers of protein powder, fat burner and other junk.

"Disgusting, eh?" he said, coming out of the bath-room and opening the fridge behind me.

He took the meat and threw it into a white oil drum that served as a trash can. There was a small card table in the kitchen and two folding chairs. Tommy drew up one of them and sat down.

"Want a shake?"

"No," I said. "Thanks." After a short silence, I asked him what we were waiting for.

"I told you, I'm working for Vincent. I've got a pack-age to deliver to a customer. Then we're out of here and I'm finished."

I had nothing to say. I suspected that something shady was going on and that Vincent's "business" was located somewhere on the wrong side of the law. But at least it was coming to an end.

We waited nearly an hour talking about one thing or another. I was trying to make a plan for the next day. We had to get on the same line so we could show what we were capable of. I promised I'd speak to Carl, the assistant coach. He'd give us a chance, I was sure of it.

Tom nodded yes to everything I said, but without much enthusiasm, as if he was only somewhat interested. Most of his attention was concentrated on the front door and the one remaining customer who was supposed to be arriving any time now.

Finally, as we sat across from each other in total darkness, the doorbell rang, shattering the silence that blanketed the spooky apartment. Tommy jumped to his feet, telling me to keep quiet and not to move.

He went to his room, opened his hockey bag and then brushed past me with a package in his hand. He felt his way to the door, hugging the wall. I couldn't see what he was doing in the dark, but I could hear him moving down the hall until he reached one of the front rooms. He returned, running.

"Quick! Hurry up!"

I stood up, not knowing what was happening or what I should do. He went to his room and came out with a backpack. My backpack, the one I'd forgotten at the gym.

"Hurry!" he told me. "Get out back. Hide yourself, I'll be there in a jiff!"

Quickly I slung the bag over my shoulder and walked out the door that opened onto a dirt yard. I slipped in the mud and wiggled through the gate and into the alley.

A streetlight shone on an old metal shed that I hid behind. And waited.

I'd grabbed the backpack with no hesitation. Now I could feel something heavy inside. After waiting for a while with no sign of Tommy, I decided to open the bag. My workout clothes were still there. Rummaging further, I felt a plastic bag at the bottom. I took it out, opened it and removed what turned out to be an awful lot of cash. In fact, it was a huge stack of twenty-dollar bills, tied with rubber bands.

A couple of juicy swear words popped out of my mouth, because never, and I mean never, would I have agreed to take off with Vincent's money. I left my hiding place set on getting an explanation from Tommy. I was about to cross the street when I saw him leave the apartment and walk toward me.

"Hey you big bozo. What's the story?"

I showed him the money.

He shrugged, hands in his pockets, shaking his head from left to right. He was sucking air and grimacing horribly. By the harsh light of the streetlight, I could see two big tears running down his cheeks.

"Come on, Tommy, what's going on? What are we mixed up in?"

"Forget it, man. There's nothing we can do."

"Nothing we can do? What do you mean there's nothing we can do?!" I shouted. "What's going on?!!"

He didn't answer, but tears were running down his cheeks. A couple of motorcycles came roaring down the adjacent alley. I tossed the wad of money right in his face and took off running.

Two Harleys suddenly appeared at the end of the alley and veered right toward me. I pivoted, and ran back to where I had started. But it was too late; a car was coming from the other direction with its headlights on. The two bikers caught up to me, jumped off their bikes and jammed my face against the metal siding of the old shed.

I recognized Vincent's sidekick, the guy with the beard, with his disgusting laugh and the red, white and blue scarf he wore on his head. Along with him was the little sourpuss who worked at the gym. He pinned me against the wall, digging his nunchucks into my throat and cutting off my breath.

"You little Indian son-of-a-bitch, one move and you're dead!"

The car crawled slowly up to where we were. It was the white Nissan Maxima with the tinted windows. Vincent got out and walked over to me, limping.

"No marks," he said to the little sourpuss, who released the pressure on my neck.

I felt oxygen begin to slowly flow into my lungs.

"You! Get in!" he shouted to Tommy who climbed meekly into the back and sat down.

Vincent stared at me. His broad face was completely red. He rubbed his forehead a couple of times as if distressed.

"Guys, guys, guys... I'm so disappointed, you can't imagine. What in the world were you thinking? Good thing Tommy was due for a shot and I came by. What do you think would have happened to you, Alex, if you'd disappeared with the money?"

His face was twisted with anger.

"Have you thought about what would have happened to you if you'd taken off with my money?!!"

The little desk clerk, egged on by his boss's words, dug his nunchucks into my throat a little harder.

"No marks!" Vincent barked, to settle things down.

He leaned over into his car for a moment and then got back out, a rectangular box covered in blue felt in his hands. He set it down on the hood and opened it, revealing the vials and syringes inside.

"Easy. No marks," he muttered to himself.

He stuck a needle onto a syringe, tightening it with his fingertips, and then inserted it into the cap of a vial to extract the liquid. After ensuring it was full to the brim, he came up to me with a demonic smile.

"I can't stand a thief. But especially if he's trying to steal from me. Normally, I give you the beating of your life. But my problem is I'm a hockey fan and I just love athletes. I know you've all sacrificed a lot to get where you are. It'd break my heart if one of you failed to reach your goal on account of something I did. That's why I like to be helpful."

And he waved the syringe in front of my eyes.

"No marks. But a good lesson for a thief and a snot-nosed brat who spies on me in my own basement. If it ever gets out that there's a doping problem on the Quebec City team, you can be sure that every one of you will be tested. What'll happen to you, Alexandre, if they find steroids in your urine?"

I didn't catch any more than half of what he said. My heart was pounding so furiously in my chest, I thought it would burst.

Vincent held the syringe just above my nose. I was sure I was going to pass out from the unspeakable horror unfolding before my eyes.

"It's too full," he said. "If I give you a dose like this, you'll end up in the hospital for sure. But what a decent man like me has in mind is for you to grow big and strong."

He squirted half the contents into my face, before lifting the needle, sticking it into my shoulder and injecting the rest. I didn't feel any pain. I was completely stunned. My legs gave out. After he pulled out the syringe and Mr. Nunchucks let go of me, I sank to my knees. The man with the beard started laughing and sputtering. Then the two bikers jumped on their Harleys, gunned the engines and took off, spinning their tires and kicking a pile of gravel right into my face.

All I could see as I looked up were the tail lights of the Maxima as it swung around the corner. In the next yard over, a dog was howling.

I walked back to my new home. It took me more than an hour to make my way up Boulevard Henri-Bourassa. I walked as fast as I could on my shaky legs, trailing my backpack, unable to get my mind off the strange buzzing sensation in my left shoulder. Everyone was asleep in the bungalow on Rue des Sureaux. I entered by the side door and snuck down to the basement on tiptoe. I could hear Louis, on the sofa bed, snoring like an old diesel engine about to give up the ghost.

Sylvie was lying on a mattress on the floor. She was awake. Fortunately, she couldn't see me in the dark. She whispered:

"Hey, you're coming in kind of late."

"Yeah."

"Did you have a good time?"

"Yeah."

"Is everything okay?"

"Yeah. Everything's fine."

I went into my tiny bedroom in the back and closed the door.

Lying there on my bed, I couldn't stop crying as I opened my laptop and looked over and over again at the beautiful pictures of Chloé. Especially the one with her eyes closed with her big smile. And the grey sea behind her. The sea, which I could practically smell and taste.

That morning the locker room was buzzing. Ties are quickly forged on a hockey team. Despite the competition, the victories and disappointments, the athletes share a passion and a team feeling evolves spontaneously. Everyone seemed in high spirits. Everyone except me and Tommy; both of us felt like we'd just come back from a funeral.

Before we went out onto the ice, Tom came over to my locker. His eyes were red, puffy. No marks, as Vincent had said. But I was pretty sure he'd been through the wringer. He didn't look too good. But my heart was cold. Bitterly cold.

"Uh ... Alex."

"Never mind, Tom. We won't mention it again, okay? It's over."

He shook his head like a forsaken puppy.

"I'm not feeling too hot. I'd better go."

"No, Tommy. This is not the time to give up. You're stronger than that. We're stronger than that. We have

to put all that behind us. We came here for just one reason, and that's to play hockey. We'll be playing against
each other today. Make sure you always come down the
ice on my side. It'll go well for you. I promise. They're
not going to be sending you home. You're going to make
the team, with me."

He smiled feebly. As if he didn't really believe a word
of it. But my pep talk must have gotten through to him;
he shook his head and said:

"Okay, let's get it going. We can do it."

"That's right, man. We can do it."

The whiteboard session seemed to go on forever. My
legs were numb. I kept clenching my jaws and rising
quickly up off the bench every time I thought the coach
had finished putting X's and O's up on the board. But
on he went and I'd sit down again, telling myself that
it'd have to come to an end sooner or later. And when
he finally laid his marker down, clapped his hands a
couple of times and shouted out two or three angry
sounding clichés, I was first out the locker room door
and onto the ice.

I went around the rink at full speed during the warm-
ups, passing Tommy several times, encouraging him
with a friendly tap of the stick on his rear.

"Let's go, buddy! Go! Go! Go!"

And he'd come after me, growling, but without ever
catching me. In fact, I stayed right up with Ruslan
Abishkin in the skating exercise and I was very proud.
No, I couldn't beat him, but I was on his heels most of
the time and I could tell he was annoyed, trying his best
to put some distance between the two of us.

I went hard at the one-on-one exercise. The coach sent a puck into the corner of the rink and two guys would battle for control. I did pretty well, giving my shoulder to guys who were a whole lot bigger than me. I might not have been the best, but I fought hard and held my own. I made some good plays that earned me some "atta-boys" from Carl.

When it was Tommy's and my turn, I eased up a bit. I decided I'd let him win. I battled hard, but without much conviction or great originality, finally letting him come out of the corner alone with the puck, like a champion.

We were side by side, catching our breath and waiting for the next instructions.

"Okay, we can do it!" Tommy exclaimed.

He was red faced, sucking wind, wincing in pain, an anxious look on his face.

"I beat you pretty good, eh?" he said, puffed with pride.

"Yeah, right on," I said, trying to put the best face on things.

Right on, Tommy, you should have seen how happy you were! You were snorting like a calf, you were hurting, my friend. But you were happy. And that was all I wanted.

The exercise period over, we formed up squads for the usual after-workout game. As I had hoped, I wasn't on Tommy's team. I was with Steven Caron and that was fine by me since I was at the top of my game and I really wanted to go up against Abishkin. Which is what happened right from the faceoff.

Arnaud, our centreman, won it. I backpedalled to pick up the loose puck, then passed it to Caron, who was coming hard after knocking over his opponent like a bowling pin. With a few sharp strides, I shook off Ruslan's tight check. As soon as I was onside, Steven passed the puck back to me. I one-timed it. Thwack! He scores!

A true work of art.

Caron, delirious, leaped into my arms, screaming for joy. It was totally over the top for a practice game, but his spirit was infectious. The guy from Maniwaki loved to compete.

I was still on the ice for the next play. In the meantime, Tommy had jumped over the boards. He was playing on the third line. An energy player, his strength was forechecking. After I made a couple of half-hearted moves, his line took control of the puck. Following the advice I'd given him earlier in the locker room, he tried to come up my side. I went at him, slightly altered direction and hit the boards behind my big friend who went to the net at full speed, with an excellent scoring opportunity. Unfortunately for him, Loïc Martin, the team's starting goalie was in net, and he wasn't about to be beat by Tommy, who tried to deke him off his feet. Martin didn't bite and easily gathered Tommy's feeble shot into his glove.

Tommy skated beside me, carrying on.

"Hey, hey, McKenzie!"

"In your face, Courchesne," I joked. "I'll nail you next time."

"Yeah, right. Go ahead and try."

It'll happen soon enough, Tom. Don't worry. I was a wicked, scary spider. A black widow, relentlessly weaving her web, knowing that her prey would end up in her net. It was inevitable.

Several minutes went by before we were face to face again, alternating shifts on the fly at the whim of our respective coaches. This time I made a real bonehead play with a sudden change of direction that let Tommy get position on me. I didn't put up much of a fight as he walked right out of the corner. He dished it off to his centre who put it right back on his stick on a nifty give and go. I could have intercepted it, but I let it go. Tom put his whole body into it and buried it behind Loïc Martin, who immediately began to harangue me, yelling that I was playing like a total wimp.

Tommy flashed his pearly whites in an outpouring of happiness. It was stacking up to be his day.

Back at the bench, Carl looked at me.

"Hey Alex, your friend get a free ride with you?"

"Last time, Carl," I answered tightly. "It's over."

"Atta boy!" And he slapped me on the back.

It was over for Tommy. Really over.

Third shift. I had just scored a beautiful goal on a breakaway on a long pass from my defenceman, and Carl left me on the ice when the lines changed. At the faceoff circle, I was shoulder to shoulder with Tommy. Arnaud won. Caron controlled the puck and passed it to me. I turned it over on purpose, putting it directly on Tommy's stick as he thundered towards me.

I gave him the right, where he had gone twice before. But no more free rides. He came on like a freight train, sure he would repeat his previous exploits. Only this time, I didn't miss.

I turned on the jets, fuelled by a dark rage. And I lined him up for a crushing check with no thought in mind other than totally demolishing him. To increase the force of the impact, with a really dirty move, I jumped and my skates were off the ice.

I could feel my back driving into his. He had twisted around, facing toward the players' bench. Right where the glass panels began. Under the force of our combined weight, he hit the metal stanchion with unimaginable force. His rib cage was completely crushed. He fell to the ice, unconscious, his body twitching in spasms.

Stunned, completely paralyzed by fear, I saw François lean over him, trying to revive him. Carl jumped on the ice with the defibrillator, and they gave him a series of electric shocks that he never responded to. He died instantly.

Eyes closed, I could sense the crowd around me, players and spectators, who had witnessed the appalling spectacle. And when I collapsed in my turn, I heard the howling of wolves bearing down on me from every direction, ripping me apart with their sharp teeth and feeding on my carcass.

Tommy, my friend, my dear friend... What happened to us? I've looked everywhere, reaching out in every direction, but I can't find any answers. I can't feel anything at all. Everything's dark.

The autopsy revealed an unbelievably high level of anabolic steroids in his body. That was why his weakened heart could not withstand the impact.

Vincent Fradette was arrested.

And as for me, I'll never play hockey ever again.